# the Forgetting Spell

## a Wishing Day Novel

# LAUREN MYRACLE

# the Forgetting Spell

*a Wishing Day Novel*

KATHERINE TEGEN BOOKS
*An Imprint of HarperCollins Publishers*

Katherine Tegen Books is an imprint of HarperCollins Publishers.

The Forgetting Spell

Library of Congress Control Number: 2016949689
ISBN 978-0-06-234209-6

Typography by Carla Weise
17  18  19  20  21   CG/LSCH   10 9 8 7 6 5 4 3 2 1
❖
First Edition

*To Lucille Glassman, who soars*

*I wish people would spend less time worrying about rules. There isn't a rule book to life, and there never will be—not if I have anything to say about it.*

—THE BIRD LADY

# PROLOGUE

When Darya was six, and hadn't yet forgotten certain things, she went off one day in search of the Bird Lady. She wasn't supposed to. She was supposed to go right home with her sisters: Natasha, who was seven, and Ava, who was only five. But Darya did it anyway, all by herself, because her life was a misery.

At school she had to sit by awful Ben Trapman, who sniffed his fingers and never washed his hair. Her desk had metal legs that squeaked. There was never enough glue to go around, and her teacher didn't like her, although she pretended to, which made it worse.

"Oh, those poor Blok girls," Miss Ellie said to

3

the other teachers. "Imagine—growing up without a mother!" And "Darya, dear, when did you last hear from her? Hasn't she written your father a letter? A grown woman—a mother!—can't simply disappear, now, can she?"

Darya hated Miss Ellie. She hated the hungry look Miss Ellie got when she peered at Darya, as if she wanted to gobble Darya up for a good story to tell the others.

On the playground—

The playground wasn't *all* bad. Last year, in kindergarten, Darya had sat by herself underneath the play structure, moving pebbles from one pile to another. She'd been so babyish.

This year, she had Suki and Stephanie to play with. Suki had shiny black hair. Stephanie had shiny yellow hair, the color of butter, and it was long and thick, and all the boys said Stephanie was the prettiest girl at Willow Hill Elementary. Sometimes they brought her Dum Dums, or pieces of gum. If it was gum, Stephanie would rip the stick into thirds and share.

Darya's hair was red and curly, and she thought maybe she would have been the prettiest girl if she was nicer, like Stephanie, and didn't pull her eyebrows together and scrunch her mouth up, like her aunts always told her not to do.

Darya and Suki and Stephanie played groundies sometimes, where you had to jump around on the play structure and never touch the ground, unless you were it and trying to tag the others. When you were it, you had to close your eyes and not peek. Suki peeked, though. Suki was still babyish about certain things. Her lunchbox, for example. Dora the Explorer!

Darya carried her lunch in a paper bag, and she packed it herself, unlike Suki, who made her mom do it. Back when Darya was four and went to half-day preschool, way back *then*, her mother had packed her lunch. Only it was called "snack," and it had to be healthy and no sweets. Mama always put a riddle in the bag, or a puzzle, folded up on a piece of paper with *xxx, Mama* at the bottom.

Darya still had those slips of paper, every single one of them. She would keep them forever, and they would be hers alone.

But today, and the day before, and even the day before that, Suki and Stephanie hadn't wanted to play groundies. They'd wanted to go witch hunting, and Darya's mother was the witch.

"Here, witchie witchie!" Suki had called during afternoon recess. She'd scampered from bush to bush, peeking under the brambles as if Mama had left Darya and her sisters and Papa just to hide on the elementary school playground.

"We should look high up!" Stephanie had said, making a sun visor out of her hand and gazing at the treetops. "People never look up. They only see what's in front of them. My mom reads mysteries every single day. That's why she knows stuff like that. If you ever have to hide from a bad guy, climb a tree, or wedge yourself high up in the corner of the ceiling."

"You can't wedge yourself in the corner of a *ceiling*," Darya replied. "How would you stay up? Super glue?"

"Or if you *are* the bad guy and don't want to be found, you should also find somewhere high to hide," Stephanie went on. "People never look up."

"My mother isn't a bad guy," Darya said.

Suki had raised her hand. She did that even when the teachers weren't there. "It was bad that she left, though. My mommy said it was *bad magic*."

Darya had pressed her fingernails hard into her palms, because there wasn't "good" magic or "bad" magic. She knew because Mama had told her so. Magic was magic, and magic was strong, and Willow Hill, the town where she lived, was chock-full of magic.

Some people said *no*, that magic was make-believe and not allowed in the real world. Even at six, Darya had known better.

"My mom said someone cast a spell on your mom," Stephanie had said on the playground.

"No, Darya's mommy did the spell," Suki corrected. "That's why she's the witch. And then she used a disappearing spell to disappear. *Poof!* That's why she's gone, right, Darya?"

And then the game hadn't been fun anymore. It hadn't been fun in the first place, really. Darya's heart ached with the sadness of missing Mama. She ached, too, from the fight of keeping the sadness *in* when it wanted so desperately to be *out*.

"Your insides are too close to the surface, that's all," her aunt Elena sometimes said when she spotted Darya being teary. Sometimes she'd go on and say, "There's no shame in it, sweetheart. Your mother felt things just as strongly."

When that happened, Darya would block her ears in her special way of humming loudly within her own head. Usually it did the trick, and after a moment, Darya could blink and lift her chin and tell her aunt that she'd had something in her eye. She hadn't been *teary*, even if it looked like she had.

Anyway, Darya wasn't like Mama.

Or maybe she was, but Mama wasn't who Suki and Stephanie said she was.

She wasn't a witch.

Mama and Papa hadn't had a big fight, which was another rumor about why Mama had left. Nor had Mama fought with Aunt Elena, who was Mama's younger sister, or Aunt Vera, Mama's older sister.

So many rumors, all of them beating their wings against Darya's worst fear: that one day, someone would stumble upon the truth. If that happened . . . well, just imagining it made Darya's tummy ball up and her legs go wobbly. What if she peed herself? A first grader! Wetting herself by the swing set, right there for everybody to see!

If Mama were here, none of this would matter. Mama would make everything better. Every day Darya wished she'd come home and do just that, but what good were wishes to a six-year-old?

Which was why she had to talk to the Bird Lady.

The Bird Lady was old and wrinkly and strange, and the rule was that Darya should be kind to her—from far away. But up close, there were different rules. If Darya saw the Bird Lady walking toward her, then Darya should cross to the other side of the street, for

8

example. Also don't wave at her, don't smile at her, and don't ever be alone with her.

But grown-ups broke rules. Mama was a grown-up, and she broke the biggest rule of all. So why shouldn't Darya?

"I need a spell," she announced, sweaty and slightly out of breath by the time she found the Bird Lady by the lake in the middle of the town park.

"Oh?" the Bird Lady said. She sat on a bench scattering seeds for the birds, but she stopped and looked Darya up and down. Flustered, Darya smoothed the skirt of the dress she was wearing. It was her happy dress with cherries all over it.

The Bird Lady's clothes weren't happy. They were strange, like the rest of her. A frumpy coat that came down past her knees and spilled over the bench, even though it was warm outside. Scuffed brown rain boots even though the sky was bright and clear.

Darya let her gaze travel higher, taking in the Bird Lady's rosy cheeks, bright eyes, and big ears with droopy earlobes. Topping everything off was a pouf of cotton candy hair, only gray instead of pink. Aunt Vera would have a fit over that hair. She'd call it a bird's nest, because of all the tangles.

A bird's nest for the Bird Lady. Darya almost

giggled. Then she remembered why she was here.

"Well?" Darya said.

"Well, what?" the Bird Lady said.

"The spell. It needs to be a forgetting spell, and I need it now."

"Ah. And what makes you think I can grant such a request?"

"Because everyone says so. That you're soft in the head and should be put in a home, but you can do things. Like spells." She furrowed her brow, bothered by a thought that before now had never crossed her mind. People in Willow Hill *did* say the Bird Lady should be "put in a home." They said it in a scolding sort of way, as if being put in a home was just the right punishment for a strange old lady with a soft head.

But wouldn't being put in a home be a good thing, if the person didn't have a home of her own?

Darya gave herself a shake. "So can you? Grant me a spell?"

"If I choose to."

"See! Then that's how I know you can, because you just told me!"

The Bird Lady tilted her head. "If I choose to, I said. Being able to do something is one thing. Choosing to do so is another."

Darya pushed twin whiffs of air through her nostrils. "Fine, then *will* you?"

"What will I get out of it?"

"Huh?"

"You want something from me. What will I get in return?" The Bird Lady's expression was cunning, and it made Darya feel . . . not naked, exactly. But something like that.

Darya fidgeted. Then she stopped, determined to prove she was a worthy match. "All right, what do you want?"

The Bird Lady tapped a gnarled finger against chapped lips. "I'm not sure you have anything I want, to be honest. You're just a child."

"I am not! I had to grow up fast, because . . . because I just did. Everyone says so, and it was very *unfortunate*." Using a word like *unfortunate* gave her courage. "And I'm smart. I've been reading since I was three. Lots of parents say their kids are early readers when all the kids can do is spell 'ice' or their own name, but I could read books and riddles and all sorts of stuff." She paused. "I was three and a half, but still."

"Riddles?" the Bird Lady said.

"And picture puzzles. I like to figure stuff out, even when it's hard. Especially when it's hard."

"You're stubborn," the Bird Lady said approvingly.

"Maybe. Maybe not."

"And ornery."

Darya scowled.

"Give me a riddle," the Bird Lady said. "Let's see if you know what you're talking about."

"I'd rather not," Darya said. Talking about riddles made her think of Mama, and she didn't want to go down that road. She very specifically wanted to *not* go down that road ever again, which was why she was here.

The Bird Lady shrugged. "Then I shan't give you the spell."

"'Shan't'?" Darya said. "Who says 'shan't'?"

"I do, obviously. It means—"

"I know what it *means*. It means *won't*, and you're being a big fat poopy head, especially since you just told me you could. You just don't want to, because . . . because . . ." To Darya's horror, her eyes welled with tears.

"If I'm a poopy head for not giving you the spell, aren't you a poopy head for not giving me a riddle?" the Bird Lady asked.

She reached into a small paper bag, which reminded

Darya of the snack bags Mama used to pack for her. The ones with riddles and puzzles in them. The Bird Lady's bag held sunflower seeds, which she scattered in a semicircle in front of her.

"I'll make you a deal," she said. "Tell me a riddle, and I'll give you the spell."

Darya squeezed her eyes shut, then opened them. "For real?"

The Bird Lady drew herself up. "I am always real, even in situations that others perceive as unreal."

Darya swallowed. This was what she had come for, after all. And she *was* stubborn. As much as she wanted to flee, a stronger part of her held firm, even though the only riddle she could think of was the riddle she hated most in the world.

"When is a door not a door?" she blurted. She gave the answer right away, afraid that if she didn't, the Bird Lady would, and their deal would be off. "When it's a jar, that's when!"

The Bird Lady looked amused.

"What?" Darya said. "That's the answer."

"Yes . . . but I'm afraid you don't know what it means."

"I do! A door is for going *out*. A jar is for keeping

stuff *in*, like fireflies. You put them in and screw the lid tight, and they can't escape because *there isn't a door.* Duh!"

"They would die, the fireflies."

"No! Not if you punched holes in the lid!"

Darya tried to get ahold of herself. She hadn't come to the Bird Lady to tell the door-and-jar riddle. She'd come very specifically to *forget* the stupid door-and-jar riddle, because it had to do with her, and Mama, and why Mama left.

Darya didn't like dead fireflies either, or dead anything. The Bird Lady was a big fat *mean* poopy head for saying that.

But clearly the Bird Lady didn't understand, so in tight, flustered sentences, Darya explained. She told the whole ugly story, and when she was done, she saw pity in the Bird Lady's eyes.

"And that's what you want to forget?" the old woman asked.

"Yes. All of it."

"You're sure? There's an old saying, you know, that you should be careful what you wish for—"

"Because it might come true," Darya finished hotly. "I know! I *want* it to come true." She clenched her fists. "I told you the riddle. Now give me the spell."

The Bird Lady studied her, and for a horrible moment Darya thought she wouldn't. That she *wasn't* a woman of her word. Then the Bird Lady cleared her throat and told Darya step by step what to do.

"*I* have to do it?! I thought *you* would do it." Darya fluttered her fingers. "You know, hocus-pocus and abracadabra."

"You, little girl, are impatient, stubborn, and prone to outbursts of emotion."

"I am not!" Darya exploded.

"These qualities can hinder you—do you know what hinder means?—but for the spell to work, you have to figure out how to let them help you. And you have to do it yourself."

Darya groaned. "This sounds like homework, and we don't even get homework yet. Not in first grade. I thought it was going to be easy!"

"Things that matter are rarely easy. Shall I tell you again what to do?"

"I suppose."

The Bird Lady raised her eyebrows.

"*Yes*. Yes, please."

The Bird Lady spoke, and Darya went straight home and followed her every instruction. When Aunt Elena asked why she needed the glue, and what in heaven's name was she doing with that shoe, Darya lied and said she was doing an art project. It was what the Bird Lady had coached her to say if anyone got nosy.

When she finished, her brain felt foggy, as if she'd woken up from a long nap. She stared out the window for a while. She pulled apart a dust bunny and threw the fuzzy strands in the trash. Soon, Aunt Vera called her downstairs for dinner. Spaghetti, which she liked, and green beans, which she didn't.

The world moved on, and Darya never realized that the Bird Lady had pulled off something clever in the casting of the spell. She'd smudged the memory Darya wanted to forget, but she'd also given Darya the key to reclaiming it, should she decide one day that she wanted to.

# CHAPTER ONE

Suki and Stephanie surprised Darya in the school cafeteria with a birthday cake, because thirteenth birthdays were special for girls in Willow Hill. Tally Striker, who was new, sat with them, her green eyes bright and curious. Darya had met Tally over the summer, and if Darya wasn't yet ready to call Tally a *friend*, it was only because Darya wasn't a new-BFF-every-day kind of girl.

She was too careful with her emotions for that.

She had trust issues, some might say.

But Tally was nice, and Steph and Suki seemed open to her, so . . . probably Tally would be a friend.

Eventually. *Maybe* already.

"You guys!" Darya said, smiling at Suki and Stephanie. She widened her scope to include Tally as well. "Thank you. You guys are the best."

"You're finally a teenager!" Suki squealed, clapping.

"For real, Darya," Steph said. "I can't believe you've been twelve for *so long.*"

"It's a stunner," Darya said. She kept her tone light, when what she wanted to say was, *Try being me. Then you'd believe.*

Every other eighth grader had turned thirteen during their seventh-grade year, or over the summer. This included Tally, who'd celebrated her thirteenth birthday before she'd moved to Willow Hill.

Darya's birthday was August twenty-eighth, four days into the new school year. This meant she'd started the year as a "tween." She'd been the lone twelve-year-old in a sea of teenagers. True, turning thirteen brought its own set of problems, at least in Willow Hill. At least if you were a girl. But Darya could go *la la la* and pretend not to think about that for several more months.

"Cake, cake," Steph chanted. "Everyone wants a piece, right?"

Darya yanked herself back to the moment. "Is Funfetti involved? Please tell me Funfetti is involved."

Steph looked at her funny. Darya couldn't figure out why until she glanced down at the cake—frosted with vanilla icing and dusted liberally with rainbow-colored stars, hearts, and moons.

"Ah-ha!" Darya said, feeling herself blush. "By which I mean, 'Heck yeah, everyone wants a piece!' Because . . . Funfetti!"

"Weirdo," Steph said, but she cut the cake without pressing the point and passed around slices on white paper napkins.

"Mmm," Darya said, taking a bite and letting its sugary sweetness wash over her.

"Should we give a piece to Natasha?" Steph asked.

Darya glanced across the cafeteria at her sister, who was older than Darya by ten months. Darya and Natasha were in the same grade at the same school in the same small town, which was—obviously—a complete and utter joy.

Ava, Darya's other sister, also went to Willow Hill Middle School. Ava was a grade below Darya. She had a different lunch period.

Darya circled the cake with her arms and said, "No. Mine, mine, mine."

Suki laughed. Steph did too, but said, "C'mon, shouldn't we share?"

She gestured at Natasha, whose long brown hair almost succeeded in blocking her from the world. She was hunched over her sandwich, taking small, methodical bites while her best friend, Molly, chattered away about something or other. The rest of their table was empty.

"She doesn't smile much, does she?" Tally commented.

"Exactly," Steph said. "Funfetti might cheer her up!"

"Or, sad but equally possible, Natasha might bring us all down," Darya said.

"Darya!" Steph said.

Darya scooped up a dollop of frosting with her forefinger. To Tally, she said, "Natasha is not . . . oh, how should I put it? Full of whimsy and light?"

Steph snorted. "And you are?"

Darya licked her finger clean. "But I don't carry the weight of the world on my shoulders. I don't get worried by everything all the time."

To be honest, Darya worried plenty. The difference was that Darya managed to hide her feelings. Usually.

Natasha chose that moment to lift her head and meet Darya's gaze from across the room. The two sisters stared at each other, until Darya, to her dismay, dropped her eyes first.

"Fine, take some over," she said, pushing her own slice away.

"Now you've made me not want to," Steph said. She lowered her voice. "I like Natasha. I really do. But—"

"*Ugggh,*" Darya said.

"You started it!" Steph said, swatting her. "Just, every so often she *does* look kind of spooky."

"She's not spooky. She's intense," Darya said, annoyed that now she had to defend Natasha.

Suki regarded Darya. "You are too, come to think of it. Intense, I mean."

"I am *not!*" Darya turned to Tally and channeled that dude from *The Terminator*. "*I. Am not. Intense. Do you understand?*"

Tally laughed. Darya smiled and took a sip of water. Her mouth was dry.

"I bet she's thinking about your Wishing Day," Suki said, tapping her lip. "I bet you are, too. Are you?"

"No!" Darya said.

"Her what?" Tally said.

"Nothing," Darya said, while at the same time Suki said, "Her Wishing Day! *Duh!*" Then she smacked her forehead. "Oh! Tally! You don't *know*, do you?"

Steph did a snap and point. "'Cause you just moved here. Right."

"La, la, la!" Darya said. "Moving on now, please!"

Tally glanced from girl to girl. "I'm confused. Will someone tell me what the heck a Wishing Day is?"

Darya groaned, because it was all going to come out. It always did. There was nothing she could do to stop it. There never was.

"Sorry, Tally," Steph said. "One of the reasons Darya gets weird about it—and Natasha, too—is because her great-great-great grandmother invented it."

"She didn't 'invent' it, and there's more greats than that," Darya groused. "She was my great-great-great-lots-*more*-greats-great-grandmother. If we're going there."

"And Darya's great-great-blah-blah-grandmother, well . . ." Suki spun circles in the air with her hand. "I guess Darya doesn't want to say 'invent,' but she made it so that there's a tradition here in Willow Hill, and the tradition's called Wishing Day. Everyone does it."

"Every *girl*," Steph said. Her eyebrows flew up. "Oooh, Tally, when did you turn thirteen?"

"April nineteenth," Tally said.

Steph moved her lips as if silently making a calculation.

"Nope," Darya said.

Steph slumped. "Bummer. You're right." She turned to Tally. "Sorry, Tally, but you're too late."

"Too late for *what*?" Tally demanded.

Suki and Steph shared a look. Then they looked at Darya.

"Okay, fine!" Darya said. "Just tell her!"

Steph perked up. "Well, on the third day of the third month of your thirteenth year—"

"*If* you're a girl, and *if* you live in Willow Hill," Suki interjected.

"That's when your Wishing Day is!" Steph said.

"Not everybody believes in it, but everyone does it," said Suki.

"Some people take it more seriously than others, that's all," said Steph. "Natasha, for example. Natasha's a true believer. Special status."

Again, Tally searched each girl's expression. She lingered on Darya. "Is this some kind of goofy initiation? Ha, ha, let's make the new girl look like a fool?"

"No!" Darya said. Shame made her feel queasy, because they *weren't* putting Tally on. "It sounds ridiculous. It *is* ridiculous."

"No, it's not," Steph protested.

"But we're not messing with you," Darya finished.

"It's just . . ." She spread her arms and smiled a game-show hostess's smile. "Welcome to weird, weird Willow Hill!"

Tally was still suspicious, Darya could tell. But her posture relaxed slightly. "So what do they believe, the believers?" She jerked her chin at Natasha. "Like your sister, for example?"

"You get to make three wishes," Steph explained. "An impossible wish, a wish you can make come true yourself, and the deepest wish of your most secret heart." She grinned. "And Darya's great-blah-blah-grandmom made it up. Pretty cool, huh?"

"No one actually knows that my great-great-great-great-great-*great*-grandmother had anything to do with it," Darya said. She had to count out the "greats" beneath the table, but she was pretty sure the others didn't see. "*Maybe* the Wishing Day tradition started with her, but maybe not."

"Oh, it did," Steph said.

"Darya's ancestors are from the *old country*," Suki said, rounding her vowels with amusement. "The old country means Russia, which is where Darya's grand-mom was from. The great-great-great one, and she had *powers*. Like, she communed with nature and tree spirits and stuff, because she was . . ." She hesitated.

"What's the word for what she was?"

"A Baba Yaga," Darya muttered.

Suki cupped her hand over her mouth. She whispered, very loudly, "Which means *witch*, but we don't say that because it hurts Darya's feelings."

Darya's face grew hot. "I'm right here. I can hear you. And Tally, I'm sure you've figured this out by now, but Suki's the one who wants to believe this crap, not me. Suki and Steph *and* Natasha."

Suki stuck out her tongue, because Suki didn't get it. For Suki, magic meant fairy tales, and fairy tales were feathery blue dresses covered in sequins, frocks she could slip over her head before twirling off in delight.

Darya, on the other hand, hated fairy tales. Fairy tales were all fun and games until someone got pushed into the oven.

"Huh," Tally said. She was skeptical, but trying to hide it.

"Yeah, the whole thing's dumb," Darya said—and she felt a pang for her quaint, embarrassing, old-fashioned town, which surprised her. Looking in from the outside, Willow Hill seemed small and silly.

"Okay," Suki said. *"But."*

Darya eyed her.

25

"*You* can say it's dumb," Suki said. "That's your right. But does your saying so make it so?"

"Um, yes," Darya said.

"*No*. You're just acting this way because of Tally. Because you're embarrassed, because your family did so start it." She shot a glance at Tally. "Darya's family has always been . . . special."

"Omigosh," Darya said, cradling her head in her hands.

"So the *tradition's* not dumb. What's dumb would be if Darya *didn't* make her three wishes, even if she doesn't believe in it," Suki said.

"Even if she feels the need to *pretend* she doesn't believe in it," Steph threw in.

"But . . . nobody's wishes really come true," Tally said. She looked confused, as if again she suspected she was being made fun of. "It's just a game. Right?"

"Right," Darya said. The not-good feelings were boiling up inside her. She tried to tamp them down.

"No," Steph said. "I know how it must sound—"

"Crazy?" Darya suggested. "Nutso, make-believe, babyish?"

"But it's not a game," Steph insisted. "We're not trying to trick you, Tally. I guess we forget how odd it sounds to the outside world."

"And the thing is, *no one knows* if the wishes come true or not," Suki added.

It felt to Darya as if her head was floating away from her body. The bad feelings were getting the best of her. "Really, Suki? Either tell the truth or don't."

Suki flinched at Darya's tone. She looked startled, and then all at once dismayed, as if immediately ready to drop the subject after all.

"*You* made *your* three wishes," Darya said, pressing forward anyway. "Steph did too. Did they come true?"

Steph touched Darya's arm. "Darya . . ."

"No, that's my point," Darya said. "Who's dumber, the two of you for believing in Wishing Days, or me for knowing better?"

Darya breathed in and out, trying to regain her control. Steph, on her Wishing Day, had set free three helium-filled balloons, after asking Darya and Suki to kiss them for luck. Then she'd whispered her wishes as she released them. Her impossible wish was for her stepfather to stop being such a jerk. The wish she could make come true herself was to persuade her mom to let her get her belly button pierced. The deepest wish of her secret heart? To be spotted by a talent scout, turn famous overnight, and have her own sitcom. She'd

27

made these wishes half a year ago.

Darya didn't know what Suki's first and second wishes had been, but her third wish had been for her boobs to grow. She'd told Darya and Steph during a sleepover, in the hushed darkness before dozing off.

"You don't *know* our wishes didn't come true," Steph said, her voice overly controlled.

Darya swallowed. "You're right. I'm sorry. I just . . ."

"You're being mean because of your mom," Suki said. She crossed her arms over her flat chest. "Because . . . well, that's the thing, isn't it? You *could* wish for her to come back."

If Suki were trying to cut Darya down to size, she had every right to. Darya kept her mouth shut and tried not to cry.

Tally shifted awkwardly.

Several tables over, a boy brayed a rude laugh.

Someone else dropped a piece of silverware, which clattered on the floor.

Darya took a shuddering breath. She glanced at Steph, then at Suki. Were they okay, the three of them? She hadn't meant to be unkind. It was all her fault.

She moved her gaze reluctantly to Tally. "What Suki means . . . it's just, my mom, she's not . . ."

"We don't talk about Darya's mom," Steph filled in.

"We don't," Suki said quickly. "And I wouldn't have, it's just . . ." Her words trickled off. "Sorry."

Darya shook her head. *She* was the one who was sorry. Her throat felt thick with held-in tears, and she marveled, not for the first time, at how much it hurt to hold emotions in. It just plain *hurt* . . . and still she did it, all the time.

Steph pushed her fingers through her hair. "Let's forget about wishes. Starting now, only happy thoughts allowed."

"That's easy," Suki said. Her relief was audible. "Cute boys."

"Four-leaf clovers," Steph said.

Tally played along, pursing her lips and drawing her eyebrows together. "Um . . . unicorns?"

Suki giggled. Steph smiled. Slowly, Darya began to come back to herself.

"Unicorns pooping rainbows," she qualified. "And friends."

# CHAPTER TWO

That afternoon, Darya went by the public library before going home. She took the longer way through the woods instead of the shorter way on the sidewalks, because she liked the woods. She liked the way the shadows played among the trees. She liked the fecund smell of the earth. *Fecund* was a new word for her. She'd stumbled across it during English, and she'd used the class computer to look up the definition.

Any other kid could have used their phone, but Aunt Vera wouldn't let Darya have a phone. Same for

Natasha and Ava. They didn't even have flip phones, not even "for emergencies only!" They were the only kids in America who didn't have phones, surely, so in that way Darya supposed Suki was right. Her family *was* special. Happy happy, joy joy.

Anyway, fecund meant fertile. It meant the dark, wet smell of soil and logs and rotting leaves. Darya liked learning new things, and she liked the discipline required to figure things out—just as she liked the nose-crinkly scent of the woods.

It was an ugly word, though. *Fecund.* It was funny how ugly words could describe lovely things, and vice versa. The world was full of smoke and mirrors. A word—or a person, or a thing—could seem one way on the surface and be totally different when you peeled back the layers and peered beneath.

The cool air of the library hit Darya as soon as she stepped inside, along with the musty scent of old books and stale perfume. She caught a whiff of paste, too, the thick gloopy kind used in kindergarten. A memory whispered from the edge of her mind—paste scooped out with something flat and wooden. One of those spoons that accompanied baby cartons of ice cream? Maybe a Popsicle stick?

Then the memory was gone, and Darya was left with a fuzziness in her head that would take time to shake off.

Darya strode past the circulation desk without looking at Ms. McKinley, whose face bulged out as if she'd had heaping servings of pudding every day of her life. Ms. McKinley wore too much perfume as well. Fake flowers mixed with baby powder, mixed with sweat.

When Darya reached the row she wanted, she ducked in and sat cross-legged on the floor. She pulled out one of the heavy yearbooks, checked the date, and pushed it back in again. She tugged a second one free. Yes, this one. The binding was creamy and substantial, and inside, the oversized pages were slick, bursting with black-and-white photos of smiling girls and boys.

*Klara Kovrov, Tennis Club*, read one caption, and there she was, her hair dark and glossy like Natasha's. A wide smile, possibly a little wild. She was glancing to the side and not at the camera, and Darya wondered, as she always did, whom her mother had been looking at. A friend, making googly eyes and sticking out her tongue to make Mama laugh? A boy she had a crush on?

Papa had gone to Willow Hill Middle School just like Mama once had, and like Darya and Natasha and

Ava did now. In the tennis club photo, Mama had been in seventh grade. Papa was two years older. When Mama was thirteen, he'd have been a freshman in high school. It could have been him she'd been smiling at, though. Who could say it wasn't?

Darya felt a tickle on her neck, and slammed the yearbook shut.

"Oh!" someone said. "Sorry, I didn't mean to scare you."

It was Tally. She was squatting on her haunches right behind Darya, though Darya couldn't make sense of it. Had Tally crept up on her? How had Darya not heard her before now? Was Tally spying on her?

Although, if that was the case, Darya had only herself to blame. Daydreaming was one thing. Getting lost in a daydream was another.

"Why are you here?" Darya asked.

Tally dropped out of her crouch and sat beside Darya, crossing her legs and scooching closer. "I felt bad about lunch. I didn't mean to bring up . . . you know. Your mom."

"*Shhh,*" Darya said.

"Oh, sorry," Tally said. "Wow, I say sorry a lot. Have you noticed?"

Darya leaned out past the shelf and glanced toward

33

the front desk. "You have to whisper, seriously, or the librarian will come charging over to shush us. Then when she sees it's me, she'll be all, 'Oh, *Da*rya, is there any news?' When she knows there isn't, because there never is."

"About . . . ?"

"My mom. Yeah."

"Well, that sucks."

Darya snorted. "Yeah."

Tally studied Darya with guarded eyes. "So what actually happened to her? I mean, if you're up for telling me."

Darya's muscles went on high alert. "I'm not."

"All right, relax," Tally said, making a *calm down* motion. "But for the record, I bet you've heard plenty about *my* mom. Am I right?"

"No," Darya lied. She tried to slow her racing heart. "All I know is that you live with, like, foster parents."

"That's all, huh? You live a sheltered life."

"And that . . . she's . . ."

"*Schizophrenic*. You can say it out loud, it's just a word. Unless—*ohhh*. Do you need me to sound it out for you?"

Darya listened with growing astonishment. "Um . . .

34

so earlier, in the cafeteria . . . what happened to unicorns pooping rainbows?"

"Nothing. Just, underneath the rainbow poop is the other poop. The *poop* poop." Tally held out her upturned palms. "We can ignore it if you want. I'm good at pretending. It's just, I had this crazy thought that maybe you were different."

Darya's mouth fell open. *This crazy thought? Did Tally just say this* crazy *thought?*

Tally hit her forehead.

"Wrong word, my bad. But since it's out there, yeah, that's one of the things I heard—that your mom went crazy." She pretended to weigh two different measures. "But schizophrenic . . . crazy . . . what's the difference? Who gets to choose, and based on what? Aren't we all crazy, at least a little?"

"*You* are!" Darya blurted.

Tally laughed. "Okay. Fine. But it *is* better talking about it like this, isn't it? I can see it on your face."

Darya almost patted her cheeks to see—or feel— what it was that she was unintentionally revealing, because it made her feel ashamed. *Tally* made her feel ashamed, and then angry. Just hours ago, she'd come around to the opinion Tally was a friend!

Then, with an amazing swiftness, a new emotion

pushed the others out. Instead of lashing out at Tally's laughter, Darya laughed back.

"You truly aren't normal, Tally. You do know that, right?"

"Normal's overrated. And again, who's to say?"

Darya considered the not-normal girl in front of her. Tally waited her out, and Darya sensed that she was summing her up, or testing her. To Darya's surprise, she realized it was a test she wanted to pass.

"Let's hear the rest, then," she said. "What other rumors did you hear about my mom?"

Tally's eyes changed. Not much else did—she didn't smile—but her eyes grew warmer, or maybe more open.

"Top runner, she left your dad for another man," Tally said. "Coming in at a very close second? She stopped taking her meds, went bonkers, and ran off 'with the fairies'—not my expression."

"My mother would have never left my father for another man *or* 'run off with the fairies'!" Darya said hotly. She felt light-headed and scared and exhilarated all at the same time, because maybe Tally was right. Maybe it was better to say these things out loud and be done with them.

"You're new here, so . . . whatever," she went on.

36

"But you're an idiot if you believe everything people say."

"Which is why I'm here. I followed you from school because I *don't* believe everything people say."

Darya held still. The walls of the library seemed to breathe, expanding and contracting.

"Oh," she said.

"Yeah," Tally replied.

Could it really be this easy, Darya wondered? Was Tally responsible for the lightness she felt, or had Darya done the unburdening herself? Or was it the two of them together, the two of them plus something undefinably *other*?

Tally gestured at the yearbook in Darya's lap. "Is it from when your mom was a kid?"

"How did you know?"

"Looks old."

Darya hesitated, then opened the yearbook to the tennis club page. "She wasn't a kid, but she was our age, yeah. That's her in the middle."

Tally leaned in. "She's pretty."

Darya flipped to another page. She watched as Tally peered at the caption.

"She won . . . what's the Academic Olympiad?"

"Some sort of school contest."

"She looks happy."

"But look at this one," Darya said. She thumbed through the pages.

"Not happy anymore," Tally murmured. "How come?"

"No clue," Darya said.

The photo showed Mama sitting alone on a bench, her expression desolate. The words beneath said, "A Moment for Reflection (Klara Kovrov, Grade Seven)."

"I bet someone thought he was so artsy, snapping that shot," Tally said.

"She *changed* that year, that's what my aunts say." She flipped back to the earlier photos. "These were from before her Wishing Day." She tapped the one of Mama on the bench. "This one was taken after. The pictures are chronological; I've checked the dates."

Tally grunted. "Do you know what she wished for?"

"Nope."

"Do your aunts? Does your dad?"

"Nobody talks about it."

Tally cut her a swift glance as if to say, *See? And therein madness lies.*

"But they think she changed because of her wishes," she stated. "Is that what I'm supposed to get from this?"

Darya floundered. She could *want* to say something, she realized, and still not know *how* to. Like, no one thought Mama's wishes had wrapped their spidery tendrils around her and squeezed her into a different shape, if that was what Tally meant. No one thought *magic* had been involved.

Except, well, her little sister, Ava, did. And every so often, Aunt Elena said things about believing in a world that was "bigger" than the visible world, and every so often, Darya almost sensed what Aunt Elena meant.

"They don't think her wishes changed her," Darya said at last. "Just that afterward, *she* changed."

"Huh."

There was a smudge on the nubbly carpet, and Darya rubbed at it.

"So something happened when your mom was thirteen," Tally said. "Something, but we don't know what, and she didn't disappear until later, obviously, or you wouldn't have been born. Not as you, anyway. How old were you when she left?"

"Five."

"Do you remember anything from then?"

Darya felt the flutter of a thought, like the flap of a bird's wing. Then it was gone, replaced by darkness and the sliding guilt of relief.

She closed the yearbook, shoved it back on the shelf, and pushed herself to her feet. She'd shared more with Tally than she'd intended to. She was surprised at how easy it had felt.

No, not easy. But natural.

Tally got up, too. "But she's not dead. No one's saying she's *dead*."

"No one's saying she's dead," Darya said softly. And yet how could anyone know?

Darya was about to ask Tally the same question, only about Tally's mom, when movement tugged at her attention. Not Ms. McKinley, but an old lady, outside the library, visible through the wide window at the back of the building. She stood half-hidden behind a dogwood tree. She seemed to be beckoning Darya.

"Tally, there's someone out there," Darya whispered.

"Who? Where?"

Darya pointed, but it was too late. The old lady had slipped behind the tree. Then, when Tally turned back to Darya, the old lady popped out again. She smiled and waved coquettishly.

"I've got to go," Darya said.

"Okay," Tally said. She kept pace with Darya as

Darya headed for the exit. "Hey, thanks for telling me about your mom."

"You're welcome. Next time, tell me about yours."

"Not much to tell," Tally said.

Darya stopped short, and Tally almost plowed into her.

"What?" she said.

She wasn't sure why she'd trusted Tally the way she had, and yet, she had. Now Tally had to trust her back, or it wouldn't have meant anything. "It's only fair," Darya said.

"Then yes, sure, whatever. I'm not hiding anything, if that's what you're thinking. Didn't we already cover this?"

"I thought we did," Darya said. "Did we?"

"Omigosh, I'll tell you now if it's that big a deal. She . . . doesn't have a family. My mom."

"She has you," Darya pointed out.

"Actually, she doesn't," Tally responded.

Darya grew hot.

"I've lived with her on and off," Tally explained with a sigh. "When I was little, she'd tell me stories. Like, about Aborigine babies being stolen from their mothers, and she'd wonder if that's what happened to her."

"Your mom's black?"

"She's almost as pale as you, so no." Tally looked at Darya funny, and Darya shrugged, though right at this moment, Darya was sure she was more pink than white. When she blushed, she really blushed.

"She also had stories about Mormon boys being driven to the edges of their towns and kicked out, or babies abandoned at hospitals, or babies abandoned on doorsteps."

"Was she any of those things?" Tally arched her brows, and Darya corrected herself. "Okay, not a Mormon boy, obviously. But I guess I'm confused. *Does* she have a family?"

"She *calls* herself an orphan," Tally said flatly. "That doesn't mean she *is*. She's been in and out of hospitals all her life, and when she was younger, she lived on the streets. She screwed up so many times that even her family gave up on her, that's what I figure."

"Oh."

"And honestly, that's the whole story, boring and predictable."

"And *sad*."

Tally nodded, but her gaze had grown unfocused.

"Well . . . that's awful. I'm really sorry," Darya said. "But, what you said. Thanks for telling me."

"Yeah," Tally said gruffly. She honed in on Darya and gave a sideways smile. "At any rate, we're basically twinsies. We can be the Missing Daughters Club."

Darya frowned. "Except *we're* not missing. Our mothers are."

Tally did the measuring-things-with-her-hands motion again. "*We're* missing *them, they're* missing *us . . .*" she said.

It took a moment for Tally's meaning to kick in. Daughters who missed their mothers. Daughters who were, therefore, in the act of missing their mothers. Daughters Missing Mothers. When the word play clicked into place, Darya felt a flare of pleasure. She *did* like figuring stuff out.

Then glumness doused the flame. She had no interest in belonging to such a dysfunctional club, and puzzles were a lot more fun when they didn't hinge on a not-so-secret sadness.

*I wish I hadn't wasted my wish on boobs.*

—SUKI KYUNG, AGE THIRTEEN AND FIVE MONTHS

# CHAPTER THREE

Tally headed back toward the middle school after leaving the library. Darya walked half a block down a side street before looping around and returning to the library playground.

"Oh, lovely," the old lady said, appearing from behind the tree. "Such a treat, Darya, dear. It's been too long, wouldn't you say?"

"No, I wouldn't," Darya said. "Too long for what, and why were you waving at me? Who *are* you?"

"Now, now, chicken," the old lady said. "You know me, and I know you. Why pretend otherwise?"

Darya opened her mouth, then shut it. She most

certainly did *not* know her, but she did know *of* her. Everyone in Willow Hill did.

She was a wrinkled old lady so ancient that no one could remember a time when she hadn't been around. She had no house, but she didn't live in the homeless shelter. She had no job, but she seemed able to take care of her basic needs, and not from begging. And she wore the most ridiculous outfits. Today, for example, she wore overalls, stripy socks, and cowboy boots.

Some people called her eccentric. Others said she stank of bad magic, and that way back when, her impossible wish had been to live forever. Others joked that actually, that was the wish she made come true herself. Only, Darya had never understood the joke.

And then there were the birds.

Everywhere the old lady went, birds followed. Right now, a robin perched on the branch of a nearby dogwood tree. A handful of smaller birds pecked at the grass beneath her. A crow stood on one of the old lady's boots, staring at Darya with one cold black eye, and . . .

Darya leaned forward to check, then drew quickly back, because *yes*. A sparrow had made a nest in the old woman's tangled hair.

"You have a bird in your hair," Darya stated.

"Can't pull the wool over your eyes, can I?" the old woman said cheerfully.

*A-a-and I'll be leaving now,* Darya thought, spinning on her heel. She was supposed to be respectful of her elders, but it had been a long day, and enough was enough.

"Yoo-hoo!" the Bird Lady said. "Come back, you silly goose!"

Darya kept walking.

"I have a secret," the Bird Lady called. "A secret that once belonged to you!"

Darya halted. She curled her toes inside her combat boots.

"It concerns your mother. I know you worry about her, pet."

Darya's heart stopped, just for a moment. She slowly turned around.

"It's been so *hard* for you, hasn't it?" the Bird Lady said, peering at her. "Hard for you, hard for Natasha, hard for Ava . . ." She tutted. "And your *father*, that poor man. It's hard for everyone, isn't it?"

"You're being mean," Darya whispered. "It's my birthday, and . . . and only happy thoughts are allowed!" Her eyes welled with tears, and the Bird Lady crumpled.

"Oh, pet," she said. "Oh, sweet girl. I didn't mean to upset you. I came here to help you!"

"Well, guess what? I don't need your help."

"Then why did you ask for it?"

"I didn't!"

"Ah, but you did. You were six years old. Your mother had been gone for . . . let's see . . . just about a year? You'd had a bad day at school, and . . ." The Bird Lady frowned, and then her eyes blazed triumphantly. "You were wearing a dress with cherries on it!"

Darya tugged at the collar of her shirt. "No. That's impossible."

"Impossible," the Bird Lady repeated. "You're fond of that word, aren't you?"

Darya started to say *no*, that of course she wasn't, and that the Bird Lady couldn't possibly know what she was fond of and what she wasn't. But things were jumbling in her brain.

The Bird Lady watched Darya keenly. "You asked me for a Forgetting Spell. Do you remember now?"

"That makes no sense," Darya said. "How could anyone *remember* a *forgetting* spell?"

"Ah, yes, another impossibility," the Bird Lady said. "You're absolutely right—unless you aren't, that is. Aren't we supposed to believe at least six impossible things before breakfast?"

Bits of first grade beat at Darya's consciousness. Warm ham sandwiches on bread with specks in it, because Aunt Vera didn't buy the good kind. Dashing around with Steph and Suki on the playground, then stopping. Watching them go on without her. Papa on the phone, again and again, and always the same words. *Klara Blok. Brown hair, brown eyes. Yes, yes.*

Papa scrubbing his hands through his hair and making it stick up in tufts. Dark splotches under his eyes. Hopelessness after he hung up, like the gloom of a dead houseplant.

The crow on the Bird Lady's boot cawed.

"Things don't always turn out the way you expect them to, do they?" the Bird Lady asked.

"Things *never* turn out the way they're supposed to," Darya said. "Not for me."

The Bird Lady laughed gently. "Feeling sorry for yourself will hardly help. If you don't like your life, maybe you should change it."

"I never said I didn't like my life."

She lifted one finger. "And another thing: Forgetting Spells last only so long. You can trap your

51

memories in a jar and twist the lid tight, but eventually they'll leak out."

Darya imagined a cluster of fireflies, which Darya used to catch and trap in empty mason jars. She imagined their fragile bodies butting against the glass. Only, fireflies wouldn't . . . leak. Fireflies would never *leak*.

"Oh, you'd be surprised," the Bird Lady said. She pinned Darya with her gaze. "And you might want to tell Tally, too. Yes, I do think Tally will come into it."

"Tally, as in Tally-the-new-girl? How do you know Tally?!"

"I don't. But Darya, dear, things always leak out."

# CHAPTER FOUR

That evening, Darya sat with her family around the long wooden table: Papa, Aunt Vera, Aunt Elena, Natasha, and Ava. At first there was a flurry of conversation—warm words for Darya, inquiries about everyone's day, please pass the pepper—and then silence settled over the group.

Aunt Vera's fork scraped her plate.

Ava burped, then giggled.

Natasha opened her mouth as if she *wanted* to say something, then closed it. She did this again, and again once more before busying herself with her noodles when Darya looked at her funny.

Aunt Elena, too, had an air of holding something in. She probably had some goofy game planned for after dinner, because they did that when it was somebody's birthday. Secretly Darya loved game night, but for the sake of her dignity, she would groan about how dorky it was.

Darya sighed. Why was nobody talking? *She* should be allowed to brood—she was a teenager now—but the others could at least try to be lively. It was her birthday, after all!

*Say something, people!* she thought. *Anyone? Anything?*

She shoveled in mac and cheese, fighting a mounting desire to . . . she didn't *know* what. Move. Scream. Flip her plate and fling her dinner everywhere, just to see what happened. At the same time, a separate part of her—distant, yet disapproving—observed her every impulse. *Judged* her every impulse, and made Darya feel as if she were a Bad Person.

*Oh, just shut up*, she told her brain, but her brain didn't listen. She wondered if other people's thoughts crashed and bounced about like this, or if she was broken somehow.

Like . . . what if she was going crazy? Or

schizophrenic. What if she was schizophrenic, like Tally's mom? When did schizophrenia kick in? Did Tally worry that she might have it?

Except Darya didn't. She was just feeling sorry for herself—as the Bird Lady had pointed out.

"Poor, pitiful Darya," she imagined well-dressed ladies saying over brunch. They'd purse their lips, and when they sipped their tea, they'd lift their pinky fingers to show how fancy they were. "Her mother *went away with the fairies*, you know."

Darya hated fairies, and she hated nice ways of putting things that weren't nice at all. And she hated tea.

*Ugh. Shut* up, *stupid brain!* She thumped her forehead with the heel of her palm.

"Darya, what on earth . . . ?" Aunt Elena said.

She hit herself again.

"Stop!" Ava said, grabbing her wrist. "You'll get shaken baby syndrome!"

"She's not a baby. She's a young lady," Aunt Vera said. "And young ladies do *not* pummel themselves during family dinners!"

"They do if they're me," Darya retorted.

"Why?" Ava asked.

"I don't know. Because I'm in a bad mood."

Aunt Vera harrumphed. "Well, perhaps if you stopped *hitting* yourself—"

"Omigosh, I stopped! Okay?" She gripped the edge of the table. "And people do get grumpy. I'm allowed to be grumpy, you know."

"But you don't need to take it out on others," Aunt Elena said.

Heat rushed to Darya's face. Aunt Elena was the nice aunt; Aunt Vera was the scolding aunt. Yet Darya had been scolded by Aunt Elena. The wrongness of it expanded inside her, and the Bird Lady's words flew through her mind: *Things don't always turn out the way you expect them to, do they?*

"You're right," she said. "I'm sorry. It's just, nothing's the way it's supposed to be."

Aunt Elena lowered her fork. "How so, sweetheart?"

"My birthday. It's not supposed to *be* like this."

"Like what?" Ava said.

"Like *this*! I don't know!"

"Has it been bad?" Ava asked.

"Suki and Steph brought you a birthday cake," Natasha said. "Suki, Steph, and what's-her-name, the new girl."

"Tally," Ava said. "The one who's so good at art. She's nice."

"Your mother liked art," Papa contributed. "She had a friend who was very good at art. Her name . . . her name was . . ." A shadow crossed his face. "I've lost it. I'm getting old."

"Papa, no," Ava said. "It was a long time ago. That's all."

There was an awkward silence.

"The cake had sprinkles," Natasha told Ava.

Ava lit up. "Oooh, I love sprinkles!"

"It was from a mix," Darya said.

"So?"

"So . . . it was made from a mix," Darya repeated. "And there were sprinkles in the cake part, not just the icing, and the colors bled and looked all smeary."

The others looked at one another, and Darya squirmed. Unwanted thoughts swirled and smeared: Mama, Tally, the Missing Daughters Club. The Bird Lady. Darya's dress with the cherries, which the Bird Lady somehow knew about.

"Are you mad because of the cake?" Ava asked. "It was still nice of them to make it, though. Even if it was smeary."

Darya hadn't thought about that dress for years, but now she saw it clearly. Vivid red spots on snowy white fabric, with a skirt that was excellent for twirling. Once upon a time, Darya had been a twirling sort of girl.

Ava waved her hand in front of her face. "Darya?"

"I'm not mad. I don't know what I am." She turned to her aunts. "Dinner was delicious, Aunt Vera. Thank you. Aunt Elena, are we going to have game night?"

Aunt Elena's eyes widened. "Oh! I'm meeting someone for coffee, actually. I didn't think you liked game night, so I thought . . . well . . ."

Aunt Elena glanced at Natasha, who shook her head so quickly that Darya nearly missed it.

"I could cancel," Aunt Elena offered.

"No, it's fine," Darya said, although it wasn't. Aunt Elena didn't "meet people for coffee." Aunt Elena read mysteries and went on long walks and came up with kooky games to play with her nieces.

"You're meeting someone for coffee?" Ava said curiously. "Is it a *male* someone or a *female* someone?"

Twin spots of pink appeared on Aunt Elena's cheeks. "Ah . . . yes."

"*Yes?* What do you mean?"

"Yes, it's a male someone or a female someone."

She rose from the table. "I better get going, or I'll be late. But Darya? I'm sorry you're having a rough day."

Natasha glanced at Aunt Elena again. Then, to Darya, she said, "Things are going to get better. You'll see."

Darya snorted. "Will I?"

Papa frowned and cleared his throat. "Sweetheart . . ."

"I'm just teasing," Darya said. "Everything's great. Everything's awesome!"

Aunt Elena hesitated, then took a step back toward the table. "If everything's great, then great. But if not, that's okay, too." She held up her hand when Darya tried to protest. "You're ready to stop talking about this. I get it. But turning thirteen is a big deal, Darya, especially in our family. Especially if you're a girl. It's . . . well, it's awfully *loaded*, isn't it?"

"Not really."

"And no matter how many lovely things are waiting just around the corner, that's not much good to you now. You said it yourself. You're allowed to feel *whatever* you feel."

"Good, because I'll probably have extra feelings, even, because of hormones. I'll probably pierce my nose and get a black-market tattoo."

"You most certainly will not!" Aunt Vera exclaimed.

"What's a black-market tattoo?" Ava asked.

"I was joking," Darya said. "Anyway, I'm pretty sure Willow Hill doesn't have a black market."

Aunt Elena laughed, which had been the goal. Yet when she did, Darya thought of Tally, and of Tally's mother, and Darya felt indignant on their behalf. Willow Hill might not have a black market (whatever a black market actually was), but some places did, and worse things than that as well.

The world was *so big*. Mind-bogglingly big, which should have given Darya perspective on how small her own problems were. Based on her admittedly limited experience, however, everyone's problems seemed big to them. Not just big, but bigger than everyone else's.

Aunt Elena gave Darya a warm hug and left, and Aunt Vera started collecting dishes. Papa got up and helped.

Natasha folded her napkin, laid it on her place mat, and rose from her seat. "Hey, Darya, since we're not doing game night, do you want to go on a walk?"

"Absolutely," Darya said. With so many things pressing in on her, the blank slate of the night sounded irresistible.

Ava hopped up. "Can I come too? Please?"

Natasha hesitated, and Aunt Vera said, "Yes, Ava. Girls, take your sister with you."

Natasha glanced at Darya, who shrugged. As long as it meant escaping for a while, it was all the same to her.

The night sky was spectacular. Willow Hill was a small town, so there were no city lights to dim the far-flung stars. A crescent moon beckoned from behind a tree, and Natasha walked toward the rope swing that hung from a high branch.

Papa had made the swing years ago. Its seat was a wooden plank, and Darya and Natasha used to swing on it together. Even after Ava came along, the three of them sometimes squeezed on all at once. Natasha and Darya would situate themselves first, before helping Ava scramble onto their laps.

Tonight, Natasha sat down at the base of the tree, among its gnarled roots. Darya joined her, leaning against the trunk and arranging her skirt to cover her thighs. Ava faced them, drawing her knees to her chest and wrapping her arms around her shins.

"That wasn't much of a walk," Darya said.

"I didn't want Aunt Vera to overhear," Natasha said.

"Overhear what?"

"What I'm going to tell you."

"Which is what? And when will you be telling me?"

"As soon as you give me a second! Sheesh!"

Darya lifted her eyebrows. She drummed her fingertips on her leg.

"The thing is, turning thirteen *is* a big deal," Natasha said.

Darya let her head fall back. "Omigosh, never mind."

"Because of your Wishing Day. Aunt Elena didn't say so, but that's what she meant."

"Still not interested. Won't ever be interested. Never not ev—"

"Will you shut up and listen?" Natasha snapped, and Darya was so surprised that she did.

"Thank you," Natasha said. She turned to Ava. "And *you*. You weren't supposed to be here for this, but here you are, so . . ." She flipped her hair over her shoulders. "You can't freak out. Do you promise?"

"I promise, yes! What is it?"

By now even Darya was intrigued, though she did her best not to show it.

Natasha gazed squarely at her. "Last year, on my Wishing Day, I went to the willow tree and made my three wishes."

*Hip-hip-hooray*, Darya considered saying. She went instead with, "And?"

Natasha's dark eyes glinted. When she spoke, Darya saw her neat, even teeth.

"They all came true."

# CHAPTER FIVE

*(before)*

Darya is in her special spot behind the curtain. Baby Ava is taking a nap, and Natasha is at preschool, probably making macaroni art. One time Baby Ava tried to eat Natasha's macaroni art, and everyone laughed, and it was the good kind of laughing, like bubbles and popcorn and fizzy drinks fizzing *every*-where.

Sometimes fizzy drinks make Darya burp, and that's another good laughing thing.

Unless Mama is in a black mood. When Mama is in a black mood, burps aren't funny. When Mama is in a black mood, nothing's funny.

Today Mama is in a gray mood, and Aunt Elena and Aunt Vera are sitting on either side of her on the sofa. Mama is the ham and the aunts are the bread. Darya wishes she could join them. She could be a pickle! Or honey mustard, which Mama likes, but Darya doesn't.

Natasha doesn't either, but sometimes she pretends. Then, when Mama isn't watching, Natasha spits out the bite with honey mustard and wads it into her napkin. When Natasha's eyes fly to Darya, they speak in invisible sister language.

*Don't tell.*

*I won't.*

*It would make Mama sad.*

*I know. I won't!*

But Natasha is at preschool, and anyway, she's bad at spying. Her cheeks go blotchy and she says "uh-oh," so Darya doesn't let her anymore.

"Klara, get ahold of yourself," Darya hears. "We don't have time for this silliness."

"Klara" is Mama.

"This silliness" is Mama's gray days.

Aunt Vera is the one who calls them that. Aunt Vera is Mama's big sister, like Natasha is Darya's big sister.

"Vera, give her time," Darya hears. That's Aunt

65

Elena, who is Mama's little sister. Aunt Elena is Mama's Baby Ava.

Mama is the middle sister, just like Darya is the middle sister.

Vera, Klara, Elena.

Natasha, Darya, Ava.

There's Papa too, of course. Papa loves Natasha and Darya and Ava to the moon and back, and the same for Mama. He calls all four of them "his special girls."

But Papa's not here, and Mama is crying.

"I can't," she says. "I just can't!"

"Klara, you can," Aunt Elena says. "You have to, for the girls."

"I made this appointment weeks ago, and you're not canceling again," Aunt Vera says. "If I have to drag you there, I will."

Mama says something, but she's got the hiccups, and her words jump around. Darya hears "Ava" and "my fault" and something about a bear. Too much of a bear?

"Klara, *enough*," Aunt Vera says.

"It's *not* enough!" Mama cries, and Darya shrinks against the wall. "Every time I look at Ava, do you know who I see?"

"Klara—"

"*Her* hair, *her* eyes. She even crinkles her nose the same way! I look at my sweet Ava, and I see *her*!"

"Klara, hush," says Aunt Elena. She's not scary like Aunt Vera, but right now her voice has wire in it. "Ava is Ava, and nobody else."

"Come on," Aunt Vera says, "up we go." There is shuffling and sniffling. "Don't you want to get better? For your daughters, if not yourself?"

"Y-yes," Mama says.

"Good!" says Aunt Elena.

"Except also"—the whisperiest of whispers—"I want to be gone."

"And do what?" says Aunt Vera. "Leave behind three little girls without their mother?"

Everything squeezes inside of Darya, and she presses her legs together.

"Pull yourself together!" Aunt Vera says. "For heaven's sake!"

Then, footsteps. Shoes with heels click-clacking away. The back door opening. The back door shutting. A car engine—*vroom!*—and tires crunching on the gravel drive.

Silence.

Good.

Only, Darya's underwear is wet. Something trickles down her legs. Only, four-year-olds don't do that, because four-year-olds are big girls. Not big like Natasha, but bigger than Ava, who *is* Ava and nobody else.

Darya bursts from behind the curtain and runs to the bathroom.

# CHAPTER SIX

"So what did you wish for?" Ava asked Natasha
in the backyard. "Omigosh. Tell us!"

"I'm not going to tell you my first two wishes,"
Natasha said. "They're private."

"But they came true? For real?" Darya asked. She
heard her skepticism and scolded herself. She could at
least hear Natasha out.

"They were dumb," Natasha said. "Which is one
reason you can't waste yours, when it's your turn."

"What was your third wish?" Ava said.

The moonlight gave Natasha's eyes an unearthly

sheen. She lifted her chin and said, "I wished for Mama to be alive."

The world stopped.

Darya didn't know how to be.

Then, with a judder—

(*cicadas, shadows, shining pupils*)

—it started up again.

"I wished for Mama to be alive, and my wish came true!" Natasha's tone sounded too bright, even shrill. "You guys! Don't you get what this means?"

"That . . . Mama's back?" Ava said with a wobble. She scanned the yard as if Mama might pop out any moment from behind a tree. Not that she was likely to recognize her if she did. Ava was four when Mama disappeared!

"You wished for her to be alive?" Darya said. "I never thought she was dead."

"Never, not ever?" Natasha said with a sharp look. She breathed out. "I didn't either, or I hoped she wasn't. But we didn't know for sure."

"*Ok-a-a-ay,*" Darya said. "So there you were, thinking maybe Mama was dead, and you wished for her to . . . what? Come back from the grave?"

Ava's eyes grew huge.

"Which, if she did, would make her a zombie,"

Darya stated. She adopted a posh voice that no one in Willow Hill would use. "Oh, don't mind Mummy. Her skin's a bit flaky, but nothing a good exfoliator can't fix. And that rotting smell? It's her new perfume. Isn't it to *die* for?"

"Darya, stop," Natasha said.

Darya bit down hard on the inside of her cheek. She didn't like how she was acting any more than Natasha did. She was horrified at herself, in fact.

"I think I need to lie down," Ava said, and she flopped back and sprawled on the ground.

"Mama's not . . ." Natasha said. She tightened her mouth, as if the word was too dumb to say. "Mama didn't 'come back from the dead,' Ava, because Darya's right. She never *was* dead." She tried to pull Ava up. "Will you sit back up, please? Darya, will you help?"

Darya scooted over, slid her hands under Ava's armpits, and pushed. Ava's shirt was damp from the grass, and her shoulder blades punched through like bird wings.

"It's a lot to take in," Natasha said once Ava was basically upright. "I know."

"It would help if you explained," Darya said. She was relieved to hear that she sounded more or less like herself again. "You kind of haven't told us anything."

71

"After my Wishing Day—well, I made my wishes in the night, but whatever—I found a note," Natasha said. "It was from Mama. Then she left me more notes. At first I thought they were from someone else, but they weren't. They were definitely from her, which is how I knew she was alive." She held up her hand to correct herself. "Which is how I knew she was *back*. She'd always been alive."

"'Back' meaning here in Willow Hill?" Ava asked.

"I asked if we could meet in person. We went for coffee."

"You don't drink coffee," Darya said.

Frustration flashed over Natasha's features. "Mama had coffee. I had a strawberry Frappuccino. All right?"

Darya drew her lower lip between her teeth. She'd wanted this forever: to have Mama back. To solve the mystery of her disappearance. To show Ms. McKinley from the library and all those other busybodies that Mama was fine, thank you very much, and that she hadn't left because she was a Bad Mother. That she *wasn't* a bad mother; she was the opposite! That Mama's reason for leaving, whatever it was, had been important.

Only, what *was* the reason? Did Natasha know?

And what if it turned out not to have been important? Would that matter? How much?

Darya's thoughts, already buzzing, flew to Tally and Tally's mother, who'd lived on the streets and maybe still did. Who invented stories to make herself feel better. Who was maybe a Bad Mother, or maybe just sick, or maybe that was just two ways of saying the same thing. In the end, she hadn't taken care of Tally, had she? Tally had been sent to live with a foster mother instead.

*Quit it,* Darya told her racing brain. *You're overthinking everything, when you don't even* know *everything. Not even close!*

Plus, wasn't she forgetting the most important part?

Mama.

Was.

Back.

Couldn't Darya just be happy?

"When can we see her?" she asked.

"Soon," Natasha said.

"Where is she?"

"At a motel."

"A *motel*?" Darya said.

"What does Papa think?" Ava said. "Wait—does

he know? 'Cause Aunt Vera doesn't, does she? Or you wouldn't have cared if she overheard. Does Aunt Elena?"

Natasha opened her mouth to respond, but Ava plowed on.

"Why did she leave in the first place? Did she tell you? And where in the world has she been this whole time?"

The silence, when Ava stopped speaking, hung heavily.

Natasha cleared her throat. "It's . . . complicated."

"What is?" Darya asked.

"All of it. It's *good*, but it's complicated!"

A screech owl called from the trees, and Darya jumped. Most people liked owls, she knew, but she thought they were creepy.

It was because of the jawbone she once found. She'd been seven, and she'd found an owl pellet in the woods, and when she picked at it, it had crumbled apart. Inside had been a tiny white bone.

"Looks like a mouse," Papa told her.

"It does not!" Darya had replied. She'd glared at him. "Mice have fur. Mice have whiskers!"

"It looks like it *came* from a mouse," Papa clarified. He ran his finger over four minuscule teeth at the thick end of the bone, then showed her the single, pointed tooth at the opposite end. That was how he knew it was a rodent, he'd said. The bone was smaller than a penny, which told him it was a mouse.

"*Used* to be a mouse," Darya had insisted.

"You guys—that owl!" Ava exclaimed. "Maybe it's a sign from Mama. She loved owls!"

"She did?" Darya said.

"According to Aunt Elena. She loved dragons, too, and princesses in tall towers, and her favorite color was sea-foam green."

"*Is* sea-foam green," Natasha corrected. She paused. "Unless it changed. People's favorite colors do change."

Darya didn't care what Mama's favorite color was or whether she liked owls.

"I asked when we could see her, and you said, 'soon,'" she said. "When is soon?"

"First I need to explain some stuff," Natasha said. "Also—about Papa. Mama's not ready for Papa to know, so you have to promise not to tell."

Darya thought of Papa's lost look at the dinner table and shifted uncomfortably. Was it right for her to promise such a thing? Then again, so much of what Natasha had shared so far made her uncomfortable!

Darya was jealous, for example, that Mama had reached out to Natasha first. That she'd left Natasha notes. That they'd met for coffee or whatever.

Darya wanted to get to the "just be happy" part.

"Fine, we promise," she said. "Now explain."

Natasha gazed at the far end of the yard, where the grass left off and the forest began.

"*Natasha,*" Darya said.

Natasha turned back. "Mama has a secret, but I'm the only one who knows. Well, and kind of Aunt Elena."

"So Aunt Elena *does* know she's back!" Ava broke in. She slapped her leg. "*Ohhh.* That's who Aunt Elena went to see tonight, isn't it?"

Natasha's eyes flew to Darya, who tried to hide her hurt feelings. "What's the secret, and why does Aunt Elena only *kind of* know?"

"Because Aunt Elena doesn't believe it's true."

"Doesn't believe *what's* true?"

Natasha hugged her upper arms. "That Papa has a sister."

There was a beat.

"Except Papa *doesn't* have a sister," Darya said.

"Papa's an only child," Ava said.

"He is now," Natasha said. "But once upon a time, he had a sister."

"No, or we would have heard of her," Ava said. "If Papa had a sister, why have we never heard of her?"

When Natasha failed to provide an answer, Ava turned toward the house, and Darya saw what she was thinking. She'd go to Papa herself. She'd ask *him* to explain.

*"Don't,"* Natasha said.

"Then stop dragging things out and tell us!" Darya said.

Natasha took a breath. "Papa had a sister. A little sister. Her name was Emily."

*Emily.* The name sent a jolt through Darya, though she didn't know why.

"Emily?" Ava said dubiously. "What happened to her? Did she run away?"

"Not exactly."

"Did she die?"

"Not exactly."

"How can you *not exactly* die?" Ava asked. "Oh! Is she in a *coma*?"

"She's not in a coma. At least, I don't think."

As they went on like this—"What do you mean,

you don't think? Wouldn't you know if she was in a coma or not?"—something nagged at Darya from the far reaches of her memory. Something dark and shadowy, and when Darya poked at it, it retreated.

"Maybe she is in a coma, okay?" Natasha said. "I don't know! What I do know is that her name was Emily, and she was Papa's little sister, and he loved her. The reason he doesn't talk about her is because—"

"No," Darya interrupted, because all at once it came to her what Natasha was going to say. Natasha was going to say that *Papa didn't remember Emily.* Only that wasn't quite right. It was more than that.

Ava looked at her, puzzled.

"Emily was Mama's imaginary friend," Darya said slowly, pulling the shadow thing into the open.

An odd expression crossed Natasha's face.

"I'm right, aren't I?" Darya said. The shadow squirmed and tried to ooze away, but Darya *was* right. She'd heard the aunts talking about it last winter, around the time of Natasha's Wishing Day.

"And Papa *does* remember!" Darya exclaimed.

"Remember what?" Ava said. "His sister, or Mama's imaginary friend?"

"Both. They're the same. Or, they're not, but that's the Emily Natasha's talking about," Darya said. She dug down deep, and it fell into place. "She wasn't Papa's sister. Mama made her up."

"That's what Aunt Elena thinks, too," Natasha said. "But it's only half the story. The wrong half."

"Then what's the right half?" Ava asked.

"Papa *did* have a sister. Her name was Emily. She was Papa's sister for thirteen years."

Darya swallowed, because Natasha sounded so certain. "And then what? *Poof*, all of a sudden she was gone?"

"And then yeah, poof, all of a sudden she was gone," Natasha said. She let out a long whoosh of air. "Mama didn't 'make Emily up.' She made her disappear."

*I wish Mama would stop acting crazy, like Aunt Vera says she should.*

—Natasha Blok, age five

# CHAPTER SEVEN

Natasha told them little more, no matter how hard they pressed, and Darya wondered if she had any clue how unfair she was being. She'd basically co-opted Darya's birthday to announce that Mama was back, only to throw in the teensy little wrinkle that *Oh, and by the way, she kind of killed Papa's little sister.*

Although, fine. Natasha never said Mama *killed* this Emily. She said Mama *disappeared* her, which made things clear as mud.

"I'd tell you more, but I can't," Natasha insisted. "Mama wants to tell you herself."

"So let's go see her right now," Darya suggested. "It's not *that* late."

"We can't," Natasha said. "It's . . . tricky." She explained awkwardly that Mama wanted to get reacquainted with Darya on her own, not Darya plus Ava.

"Hey!" Ava protested.

"She wants time with you, too!" Natasha assured her. "Just not at the same time. Not this first time."

After going around in circles for several more minutes, she made the Official Big Sister Proclamation that they'd talk more in the morning, and she rose and headed for the house. Darya assumed they truly were going to bed, and though she was frustrated, she called out "good night" and "love you" as the three sisters retreated to their separate bedrooms.

Five minutes later there was a soft rap on her door.

"It's me," Natasha said, slipping into Darya's room and easing the door shut behind her.

"Yes, I can see that," Darya replied.

Natasha was already in her flannel nightgown, because Natasha was that kind of girl. She settled beside Darya on her bed and said, "The thing is, we can't hurt Ava's feelings."

Darya didn't like Natasha's ownership of Mama's return. She didn't like Natasha's smugness, either. It wasn't on purpose, Darya had no doubt. But that only made it worse.

*I am the oldest, and I know things*, Natasha's concern suggested. *Mama chose me to first reveal herself to, after all. It's quite a responsibility.*

"I have no intention of hurting Ava's feelings," Darya said. "Let's sneak out now. You know how quickly she conks out."

"It's more than that. Mama *does* want to see you— so much! But she needs time."

Darya groaned and fell back against her pillow. "She's had time. She's had *eight years*."

"She wants to take things slowly."

"How slowly?"

"She wants to be ready. She's nervous."

"Well, so am I!" Darya exploded, not realizing she was on edge until she said it.

"Then see?" Natasha said. "It's for the best, for both of you."

Darya flung her arm over her eyes and groaned again.

"I'll take you to her next weekend. Papa has an art festival to go to, and Ava's going with him. You can wait till then, can't you?"

Darya moved her arm just enough to eyeball her

sister. "Do I have a choice?"

"Well . . . no. But the week'll pass in a flash, and then you'll see Mama, and it'll all be worth it." Natasha stood up, and the mattress jiggled. "Good night for real. And . . . oh yeah. Happy birthday."

# CHAPTER EIGHT

Darya had kept the tiny mouse jawbone, the one she'd found in the owl pellet. She'd washed it and put it in an empty spice jar, which she'd hidden behind a row of books on the highest shelf of her bookcase. She was well aware that some people, possibly most, would consider her to be the creepy one, while continuing to coo over the darling sweet owls who ate the mice and digested the flesh and left the bones behind.

Darya spent little time worrying about it. It wasn't as if anyone knew. And if nobody knew, then who's to say it was true?

That went for most things, not just mice bones.

Before she fell asleep, she dragged her desk chair over to her bookshelf and climbed up on it. She pulled five books from the top shelf and stacked them on the shelf below. She reached through the gap and felt around until . . . *there*. She felt smooth glass and she drew out the spice jar.

"Hi, little mouse bone," she said in her quietest voice. "I hope you're happy, wherever you are." She meant the mouse, or rather the mouse's soul, and not the bone itself.

She thought of Mama.

She thought of Papa.

She didn't make a birthday wish, because . . . she just didn't.

But she closed her eyes and kissed the jar, and knew it was practically the same.

# CHAPTER NINE

Darya had grown up missing her mother. It was part of her identity, so in that way, maybe Tally's Missing Daughters Club was aptly named after all.

Darya had longed for Mama when she needed her first bra, and Aunt Vera had taken her to buy one, even though Aunt Vera was the worst person in the world to go bra shopping with. Even worse than Papa. With Papa, there'd have been embarrassment, but he'd have let her choose whatever bra she wanted. Aunt Vera had bought Darya three identical bras, each one *beige* and each one ugly.

When Darya got her period, she'd at least had Aunt

Elena, who wasn't afraid of talking about things. And she'd had Natasha. Still, she'd yearned for Mama.

She'd wanted Mama when she got a D on a sixth-grade math test and Mr. Barnes made her stay late after class. He'd been kind about it, and she'd gnawed the inside of her cheek to keep from crying. For days, her tongue had gone compulsively to the ridge of wounded flesh, prodding and exploring.

She'd wanted Mama when she got an A-plus on a project about sea turtles. When a baby sea turtle got stuck inside its egg, it was called "half-pipped," Darya had learned, and she'd known that Mama would have liked that. Darya had never been to the beach, but she'd imagined rescuing a half-pipped baby. She'd have kept it safe in a cool, dark place until it was strong enough to live on its own, and when it was time, she'd have taken it to the edge of the shore and watched it make its way into the sea.

*Oh, my baby girl,* Mama might have said, standing barefoot in the sand and squeezing Darya's shoulders. *I'm so proud of you.*

Missing Mama was hardwired into Darya's soul. But when she woke up Saturday morning and remembered that Mama was in Willow Hill and close enough to touch (if only Natasha would take Darya to her!), the missingness throbbed with almost unbearable intensity.

She needed to distract herself, so she called Tally to see if she wanted to go out for coffee. Not real coffee, more like a coffee-ish drink of some sort. Even a strawberry Frappuccino, although Darya preferred mocha chip.

But Tally's foster mom told her that Tally was at the art studio at their middle school, because Tally was awesome that way. Tally's foster mom didn't say that last part, but it was true. Darya had met Tally in a summer art class—it was supposed to be jewelry making, but it turned out to be "Sketching in Graphite" or something equally unshiny—and Darya had quickly learned that Tally was the real deal.

Whereas Darya thought about how cool it would be to make art, Tally went out and actually did it. Or made it. Or whatever.

Maybe Tally had inherited her talent from her mom? Maybe being an artist was something the two of them shared?

Mama hadn't been a visual artist, but she had been creative. Darya remembered that. Stories, word puzzles, and picture puzzles too, come to think of it.

So maybe Mama *had* been good at drawing. Maybe

she still was. Maybe being an artist could be something Darya and Mama shared, and it could be their thing. Natasha wasn't any good at drawing. Ava? She wasn't bad, but dancing was more her thing.

*Go do it, then. What's stopping you?* Darya thought.

(*Oh, my talented girl,* Mama might say when Darya brought her a brilliant drawing of . . . whatever. *I'm so proud of you!*)

And yet a sucking lethargy held her back. Gathering pencils and paper seemed like such a lot of work. Finding something to be inspired by seemed like such a lot of work. Anyway, anything she drew would turn out stupid. She had decent ideas sometimes, she thought, but the few sketches she'd completed were massive failures.

For example, she and Ava had gone on a picnic over the summer. It was after the jewelry-making class turned out to be an art class, and Darya had an assignment to complete. "Draw something from nature" was the gist of it, so she'd headed out to get inspired.

The air had smelled like apples, and the sky had been an enormous placid lake. They'd drunk lemonade from a thermos and shared a package of sweet, crunchy cookies shaped like windmills, which Ava wanted more and more and more of.

She made grabby fingers and said, "Hand over the cookies now, you cookie hog, or I'll run off in tears!"

Only Darya heard "or I'll run off in *deers*," and she imagined a girl running down a hill, but with hooves instead of feet. She'd have velvet ears sprouting from flowing hair, and she'd run with widespread arms, her fingers flinging out a trail of deer after deer after deer, each one smaller than the one that came before.

Ava, running off in deers.

At home, Darya tried to draw it, but what came out was flat and potato-ish and captured nothing of Ava at all. Or of deers. She'd ripped the picture to shreds, then burned the shreds, then flushed the charred bits as well as the match down the toilet. Ava, swirling away in smears.

Even so, Darya *could* go and join Tally today. Ms. Meade opened the art room to students over the weekends if they respected the space and didn't mess anything up. Maybe, with a few tips from Tally, Darya could manage to draw a brilliant picture for Mama.

But Tally was *so good* and Darya was *so bad*. What if, deep inside, Tally felt embarrassed for her? What if she pitied her?

Or . . . *shhh* . . . what if, deep inside, Darya wanted

to see Tally for an entirely different reason? What if, deep inside, Darya wanted to let it slip that *her* missing mother might not be missing anymore?

Darya would despise herself if she acted on that impulse, and Darya despised herself far too much already.

She called Steph, who answered on the first ring.

"Darya, hi!" she said. "Omigosh, I would *love* to talk, but—hold on, Mom! I'm coming!—my mom's taking me shopping." She must have heard the brightness in her voice, because she quickly toned it down. "It's going to be so boring, but I already said I would."

Darya took a sort of mental deep breath and reminded herself that fair was fair—and also, wow, mommy issues popped up everywhere. Whereas Tally had a crap relationship with her mom, Steph got along with hers almost too well. If anything, Steph downplayed how good their relationship was the way certain girls downplayed their size-zero figures by pinching their tummies and bemoaning their nonexistent fat.

Except what the skinny girls were saying, without words, was, *Why yes, I* am *skinny, even if I pretend I'm not. Go on, then. Envy me.*

What Steph was saying was more along the lines of, *You don't have a mom, which is really super sad, and I don't know what to do about it. Maybe it'll help if I pretend you're not missing out on much?*

"Steph, you love going shopping," Darya said.

"I do?"

"Have fun. Buy lots. Just resist the leopard print thong this time, 'kay?"

"Ew."

"Don't let your mom get one either," Darya said.

"Ew!" Steph said, but she laughed, and Darya hoped Steph heard what she was really saying, which was that she was fine with Steph having mother-daughter bonding time. More than fine!

She wished she could tell Steph about Mama, but if she told Steph then she should tell Suki, which brought back the question of telling Tally, and . . . not yet. *Soon*, she told herself. The missingness burned as intensely as ever, and frustration, too. Resentment that she'd been forced to miss Mama for so long?

Forget that. The end was in sight, and the excitement kept Darya from going under.

She tried Suki after she got off the phone with Steph, but the call went to voice mail. Suki was probably at church with her parents and little brothers. The Kyungs went to church a lot. There was a potluck every weekend, it seemed. Lots of orange fluff marshmallow salad, although Suki had confided that it wasn't technically a salad.

"It's served on lettuce, which is maybe why they call it a salad," she'd told Darya, in the hushed voice of someone sharing a very important secret. *"But no one eats the lettuce."*

"Ah," Darya had said. "Sneaky."

Suki had nodded. "I know, right?"

Darya hung up without leaving a message, although again, she ached to share her own sneaky news.

*Ugh*, she was driving herself crazy.

No, not *crazy*. Double ugh!

But she needed to get out of the house. She needed to move!

She went outside, dashed across the yard, and continued through the taller grass beyond, mounting a slight hill and skittering down the opposite bank. It was hot, and sweat pooled at her hairline and on the small of her back. She was breathing hard when she reached the field of wildflowers she loved so much.

She propped her hands on her thighs, bending over until her heart stopped hammering. She lay down among the flowers and reached out to Mama with her mind. She tried to remember every single thing she could about her, but her memories were slippery silver

96

fish: darting here, then there, then *whoosh*, gone in a flash if Darya got too close.

Did Mama have the same problem, or did Mama remember every last thing about Darya?

That's what mothers were supposed to do. Good mothers, anyway. Steph's mom surely did. Suki's mom too, Darya suspected. Tally's mom?

Better not go down that road.

Better, perhaps, not to lump mothers into "good" versus "bad," period. Maybe, to use Natasha's incredibly annoying word, things were more *complicated* than that.

Or not.

Darya closed her eyes and let the sun anoint her skin, and it crossed her mind that maybe, at the most basic level of all, mothers and daughters were just . . . people. Darya didn't know where she was going with this thought, but once upon a time, Mama had been a daughter. She'd also been a student, a friend, a baker. A wife.

People were people. A single label was too small for anyone.

And yet . . . *mother*. Wasn't that a bigger label than most? Darya knew that being a mom wasn't *all* a woman who had children was supposed to be. She could still try new chocolate soufflé recipes and solve math problems and have a career, whatever. But wasn't the "being a mother" part supposed to be really, really high on the list of what to focus on?

Like, take Tally's mom. Darya didn't mean to think this, she didn't, but why couldn't she *make* herself get better? Darya understood that Tally's mom had some kind of mental illness, and that wasn't her fault. But there were doctors, right? And medications? If a doctor told Tally's mom, "Do this, and you'll feel better and be able to take care of your daughter," why wouldn't she?!

BUT THEN.

On the other hand, why would a mother *leave*?

Darya had heard the same rumors Tally had, that Mama had gone a little crazy in the days and weeks and months before she disappeared.

So possibly Mama and Tally's mom *both* had some sort of mental illness.

Darya blinked in surprise, because she found that it was much easier for her to feel forgiving of Mama— *if* Mama was mentally ill—than it was to have a soft heart toward Tally's mother. That wasn't cool. She vowed to not be so judgy about things she didn't fully understand.

But when it came to Mama . . .

In the big picture, it didn't matter, because Mama *didn't* have a mental illness. To say someone had gone "a little crazy" was just a figure of speech.

She tried, as she'd tried before, to feel her way into the murkiness that *crazy* dredged up. And by *crazy*, Darya meant a teensy version of crazy, as opposed to "diagnosed, for real, with a chemical imbalance or some sort of syndrome."

Like . . . eccentric crazy! That kind!

For example, what if Mama said that olives were delicious—

Or no, because olives truly were disgusting.

So, orange fluff marshmallow salad. She yawned, but stuck with it. If Mama said orange fluff marshmallow salad was all kinds of delicious, and everyone else in the world said, "No, it's *awful*," that would mess with her after a while. Wouldn't it?

If someone told Darya that *poison* was delicious, or dog food, or poop, Darya supposed she might think that person was a little on the crazy side.

A breeze ruffled Darya's hair, and she curled onto her side and rested her cheek on the pillow of her hands.

*You're safe*, the violets whispered.

*Shhh*, crooned the forget-me-nots. *Shhh, shhh.*

99

Long ago, when Darya told Mama about how the flowers talked to her, Mama'd said, "Of course they do, sweet pea."

Then.

After.

After Mama left, Darya had walked to the mailbox with Aunt Vera one afternoon. Darya said something about how chatty brown-eyed Susans were, and Aunt Vera had stopped in her tracks. Aunt Vera had glared at the brown-eyed Susans, who fell silent. Then Aunt Vera had glared at Darya, and the pressure in her chest told her she'd done something bad. Next came shame, hot and heavy.

Aunt Vera's lips had folded in on themselves, and Darya'd heard the words she didn't say.

Flowers didn't talk.

Little girls certainly didn't hear them if they did.

But Darya wasn't so little anymore, and she got to decide, didn't she? What to believe and what not to believe?

*Shhh*, the violets said.

*The sun is warm.*

*The air is sweet.*

*Rest for a spell. All will be well.*

*We wish for sun and rain and rich, moist soil.*
*We wish these things for her.*
—THE VIOLETS

*We wish for her to remember.*
—THE FORGET-ME-NOTS

*We wish for her to know.*
—THE BROWN-EYED SUSANS

*We wish for her to grow.*
—THE GRASS

# CHAPTER TEN

*(before)*

Mama is having a gray day, and there is a sour smell in her room that makes Darya's nose crinkle. She wonders if she was wrong to knock on the bedroom door, and wrong to push on in when Mama didn't answer. Maybe she should have kept on working with clay at the kitchen table, with Natasha.

The clay is salt and flour and water all mixed up, and the smell it makes is heavenly. The feel of it on Darya's hands is heavenly, too. It's still there even after Darya washed up, because she didn't wash up *all* the way.

Darya brings the back of her hand to her nose and breathes in, and she thinks it makes the sour smell go away a little bit. She does it again, for courage, because Darya is the brave sister. It's her job to cheer Mama up. Natasha won't, because Natasha is the good sister who does what she is told. Ava's only three, so no one knows yet what Ava is, except that she likes to squeeze handfuls of applesauce in her chubby fists. She likes the way it squelches out, which Darya understands. It's that same way with the clay.

And then Darya thinks that Ava is the clay sister! Because she hasn't been molded yet. She's still being squelched out!

Darya laughs, and Mama says, "Is that you, Darya?"

She's in bed with her quilt drawn tight. Her hair is greasy, which Darya doesn't like. She likes Mama's soft and shiny hair, not this greasy hair that lies on the pillow flatly.

"I made you an art project," Darya says. She steps closer. "It's called 'Autumn.' That's the *theme* Miss Annie gave us, and Thomas didn't know what *theme* meant, so Miss Annie had to tell us. It means what you want your art project to say. Do you want to see my art project, Mama? Should I get it?"

"Baby, I would love that," Mama says. Her voice is tired, but it's a yes and not a no, so Darya knows her idea was a good one. Mama loves art. Maybe Darya's art project will make Mama come back from herself, and everything will be sunny again.

"I'll get it. I'll be right back." Darya pivots on her heel, then turns around again. "Only, do you want to see the one I did for Miss Annie or the one I did for myself, out of the clay Natasha made for us?"

"Natasha made clay?" Mama smiles. "What a good sister. You're lucky to have such a good sister. Do you know that, Darya?"

"I'll get them both," Darya says. "I'll be right back." She leaves with quick steps and pretends she doesn't hear when Mama calls for her to close the bedroom door, please, it's letting in too much light.

She thumps downstairs and grabs her art. The preschool one is on a piece of construction paper. It's crumpled a bit, but Darya doesn't mind because she doesn't like it anyway. Or, she *did* like it at first, but Miss Annie said she didn't do the theme right, and that changed things.

She puts her bits of clay on top of the drawing and lifts the drawing by the sides, so that it's a basket and the clay bits are the picnic treats inside. Only they're not picnic treats. That's silly. But clay would be good for making picnic treats, if the theme was picnics.

She hesitates, thinking what a nice pea she could

make if she sat back down at the table. One canoe-shaped bit for the pod and three rolled-up balls for the peas inside the pod. It would be easy! She wants to touch those three little peas she hasn't made. She wants to roll them in her palms until they're just the same size and just the same roundness.

But Mama is waiting, and also Natasha is talking to her. She's saying, "You're not supposed to bother Mama. Papa said. She's napping and we're to leave her alone."

"You leave her alone," Darya says. "I'm going to show her my art." *And I'll make the peas and the pea pod later*, she tells herself. And a carrot, and a sandwich—a sandwich would be fun—and a cookie, with bumps and pinched bits to show that it's chocolate chip. Then she'd have an autumn theme *and* a picnic theme. She can do whatever themes she wants, without Miss Annie to say, "You did well, Thomas!" or "Oh, Darya, you've put in quite a lot of effort. I can see that. But it's not exactly autumn you've drawn, now is it?"

Back in Mama's room, the hallway smell and the staircase smell and a little bit of kitchen smell have made the sour smell better.

"This is my preschool one," Darya says, putting the

clay to the side and handing Mama her drawing. It's on a red piece of paper, and she used crayons to draw lots of little girls, all of them in star shapes, like they've been caught in the middle of doing jumping jacks, or cartwheels. Only the girls look more like blobs than stars. Also, the girls' hair—which was supposed to be in doggy-ears—looks more like messy scribbles.

"They're falling out of a tree," Darya tells Mama, "except I didn't draw the tree right."

"Is this the tree?" Mama says, touching three long lines on the side of the paper.

"Miss Annie thought it was a zucchini! And the girls are the leaves, and that's why it's autumn—because autumn is another name for fall. But Miss Annie said my effort wasn't good enough."

Mama studies the drawing. She really studies it, sitting up a bit in her bed and pushing her hair behind her ears. "It's a picture puzzle," she says. "You have to put the pieces together to figure it out, but that's what makes it so wonderful. I love it, Darya."

Darya is whooshed up by happiness. The puzzle pieces inside of her come together just like the puzzle pieces of what she drew, and everything feels right again.

"Do *you* think I did the theme right?" she asks Mama, to make sure.

"I know you did," Mama says. "Can I see what you made from the clay?"

Darya scoops the bits from Mama's dresser where she dumped them. She spills them onto Mama's lap.

"This is the girl, and she's better, isn't she? Than in the drawing?"

Mama turns the girl around. Darya used a cookie cutter. That's why it worked.

"These are the leaves, and see these holes?" She made the holes by digging a pencil tip through the clay and going swirl, swirl, swirl. "That's so I can hang them up, after I make a tree."

"How will you make the tree?"

"Twigs. And glue."

"Will the girl be falling from the tree, like in your drawing?"

"Yes, but better. I haven't figured out how, but yes."

Mama smiles, and Darya feels her own face burst into a grin.

"You have big plans."

"Uh-huh. I wanted all that to be in the drawing, but . . ." She pushes her breath out. "Miss Annie couldn't see it."

Mama lifts her chin. "Well, *I* can. Would you like to know what else I see?"

Darya nods.

"I see a little girl with a huge imagination, and I wonder what her story is. I wonder what she's already done, and I wonder what she's about to do. I see the whole world unfolding before her."

Darya holds still, letting those nice things wash over her. She soaks in all the Mama-ness she can.

"Do you have a blank piece of paper?" Mama asks. "And a pencil?"

Darya doesn't, but she can get them. She returns and gives Mama a piece of notebook paper, a freshly sharpened pencil, and a hardback picture book to bear down on. Mama didn't ask for that last thing, but she nods approvingly.

The book is *The Ice-Cream Cone Coot and Other Rare Birds*, which Darya loves, even though it scares her. It's full of pictures of birds that aren't real, not like the bluebirds and thrushes that perch in the trees in the backyard. The book pretends they are real, though. Like the Garbage Canary, who has a trashcan for a body, or the Cupadee, which is a teacup on legs. Like the Jackknife Niffy, which is described like this:

*I do not trust the Jackknife Niffy. He could swoop down and cut off your nose in a jiffy.*

The Jackknife Niffy gives Darya the shudders, but she can't *not* look at it when she reads the book. Right now is not book-reading time, however. Darya watches curiously as Mama draws a tilted glass with a heart spilling out of it. She turns the picture toward Darya and says, "Can you see what this is?"

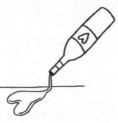

"A bottle with a heart coming out of it," Darya says.

"Yes, but it means something more than that, too. Try thinking of it in a different way."

Darya studies it. She tries really hard. "A wine bottle with a heart coming out of it?"

"The expression is 'Pouring your heart out.' Have you ever heard that before?"

"No. Maybe?"

"Let's try another." Mama draws something new. "Think of it like a puzzle, like the picture you did for Miss Annie. The theme was autumn, and you drew a girl falling out of a tree, because 'fall' is another word for 'autumn.'"

She twists the paper toward Darya. This one is just

words, but they're squished together and one is bigger than the others.

yourLUMPthroat

"Any thoughts?" Mama asks.

"Your lump throat," Darya says.

Mama smiles, and that makes Darya feel good. Except Mama doesn't say, "Good girl, well done!" She says, "When you cry, what does it feel like?"

"Sad?"

"Yes, but what does it feel like in your body?"

Darya doesn't want to get it wrong. "Um . . . tearstained?"

"Hmm," Mama says, and Darya squeezes her hands into fists. She does feel tearstained when she's sad. She feels like she might feel tearstained soon, but she fights against it.

Mama points at the word *lump*. "What's this word?"

"Lump."

"Right! What's it in?"

"What's it *in*? What do you mean?"

Mama covers "lump" with her finger. "What does it say now?"

"Your throat."

"Right again!" She moves her finger. "So the *lump* is . . . ?"

Darya stares at the puzzle. She thinks really, really hard, so hard, and then suddenly, the fog in her brain goes away—and she hadn't even known she'd had fog in her brain. "Lump in your throat! Is that what it means? Did I get it right?"

"You did. Very good!"

"Do another," Darya says, because she's beginning to understand. She can't look at Mama's puzzles the normal way, or she won't figure them out. She has to look at them sideways, kind of.

Mama taps the pencil against her chin, then scribbles on the paper. She shows it to Darya, saying, "You are getting so smart that people are going to think you're this."

# ENCYCLOPEDIA

Darya peers at it. First she has to sound out *encyclopedia*, which is a big word even for a "precocious" reader like herself. Then she tries to figure the puzzle part out. Is it an encyclopedia wearing shoes? No, because that doesn't make sense. Darya is learning that the puzzles have to make sense for them to work. And she'll know when the answer makes sense, she thinks, because . . . she'll just *know*. Because that's what making sense means. Because when a puzzle piece fits, it fits.

And then the fog clears, and it happened so much more quickly this time.

"A walking encyclopedia!" she crows.

Mama laughs. "Very, *very* good, Darya. Not everyone can think outside the box, but you can." She cocks her head. "That's a pretty awesome skill, you know. I think you're going to be just fine."

Darya smiles, but she doesn't understand.

"One last one," Mama says, and she makes the pencil fly over the paper.

Darya scrunches her mouth. "Hmm," she says, just like Mama said earlier. "*Hmm.*"

She thinks of different answers, but none has the right rightness to it. Then, all at once, the answer clicks into place. "Catching some Z's!"

"Well done, Darya-potato," Mama says. "And now, that's what you need to let me do."

"What do you mean?"

"I'm tired, sweetheart. Let me rest." She yawns and gestures to Darya's bits of clay, which are on Mama's bedside table. "Don't forget to take your art project."

Darya gathers them up. They need to dry, anyway. For two whole days, they'll need to dry, because that's how long it takes when they have to air-dry.

Using the oven would make it quicker, but Darya and Natasha can't use the oven. They're just kids.

Mama can use the oven, because she's a grown-up. But she's having a gray spell.

For a little while, it seemed like the gray had lifted. But, no.

Darya tiptoes out of the room and closes the door behind her. She never does finish her art project, the one with the clay and the tree made out of twigs and the little girl hung to look like she's falling. She and Mama keep doing picture puzzles, though. She gets better and better at thinking outside the box, and when Mama gives her the picture puzzle for that expression, she solves it in a jiffy.

THINK

# CHAPTER ELEVEN

Monday arrived, and Darya was jumpy with anticipation. She'd be meeting Mama in *five days*. Well, not meeting her—Mama was Mama; Darya "met" her on the day she was born and lived with her for five years afterward—but meeting her *for real* as a teenager, and she vacillated from desperately excited to petrified to foot-twitchingly impatient.

Round and round went her thoughts, just like in the song kids used to sing in kindergarten. *'Round and 'round the mulberry bush, the monkey chased the weasel. The monkey thought 'twas all in fun . . . Pop! goes the weasel.*

She kept busy, hoping to make time pass faster. She went home from school with Suki a couple of times, and Suki used a new kit of hers to give Darya a "gel manicure." After Suki painted her nails, she had her stick them into a machine that blasted them with ultraviolet light. When Darya pulled them out thirty seconds later—"Thirty seconds! That's all!" Suki exclaimed—they were dry.

"And guess what?" Suki said. "The polish'll stay on for ten to fourteen days. No chips or anything."

That evening, while Darya was opening a Dr Pepper, the sparkly blue polish on her index finger came off. It fell away in a single, perfectly formed oval.

She pried at the polish on her other fingers, and *pop-pop-pop-pop-pop-pop-pop-pop-pop*. She was the proud owner of ten creepy fake nails, like the fingernails of a girl who sank to the bottom of a freezing lake and died.

With Steph, who was in Darya's algebra class, Darya passed notes back and forth about Benton Hale, whom Steph had a crush on. Lots of girls had crushes on Benton Hale. Last year, Natasha had been one of them, and for a short while, he seemed to like her back. He'd possibly sent her secret admirer notes, Natasha had told her sisters. But then, after Natasha finally got up the nerve to thank him, he asked her advice on how to impress another girl!

Except—*crap.*

Darya, all these months later, realized that maybe history needed to be rewritten.

*She left a note for me,* Natasha had told Darya on Darya's birthday, and by "she," Natasha had meant Mama. Natasha said Mama left *lots* of notes for her, and that at first she thought they were from someone else, but it turned out they weren't.

Darya made a mental note to ask Natasha if the notes from Benton were actually from Mama.

Darya spent extra time with Tally as well, hanging out with her in the art room and trying halfheartedly to create something magnificent. It was hopeless, of course. Tally was infinitely more talented than she was. Tally didn't rub it in, though. She didn't bring up Darya's mother again either, and Darya returned the favor by not bringing up Tally's mom. They had an unspoken understanding, it seemed.

There were a couple of times when the two girls were working side by side, but not talking, when Darya considered sharing the secret of how Mama was back and how Darya would be seeing her in just a few days.

But she didn't.

So.

She nursed a secret fantasy, though. A week or two from now, once Mama got all the way settled, maybe Darya could invite Tally over and let her see for herself that Mama had come back. No big drama, just everything the way it should be.

Mama would smile at Tally and offer both girls cookies hot from the oven, and Papa would be there, too, humming and giving Mama a quick squeeze every time he passed her, just because he could. Darya wouldn't rub it in, though, her happy, back-to-normal family.

⌒

On Friday evening, Aunt Elena found her after dinner. "I was hoping we could talk," she said, after knocking on Darya's door. "Do you have a minute?"

"Sure," Darya said.

Aunt Elena took a seat on Darya's bed. She smelled delicious. Aunt Elena always smelled delicious. She had twenty different bottles of perfume, easily.

She bit her bottom lip, then met Darya's gaze and smiled. Darya smiled back, quizzically.

"Natasha told me that she, ah, gave you the news?" Aunt Elena said.

Darya checked that her door was shut. In a soft voice, she said, "About Mama? Yeah, I'm going to see her tomorrow. I wanted to earlier, but Natasha said it would be better if we waited." She remembered Aunt Elena's departure after her birthday dinner. "You've seen her already?"

A smile broke over her face. "It's wonderful having her back. She's my sister, after all. Can you imagine a life without Natasha or Ava?"

"No, and I don't have to, because that won't happen."

"Of course not. Although I'd have said the same, back when you girls were younger . . ." She let her sentence trail off, then found the end of it and started back up. "But no, you're right. At any rate, that's not why I'm here. I'm here to tell you some news of my own."

"Okay."

"It'll be a change for all of us, but a *good* change, I think." She swallowed. "It's not that big of a deal. Just, I'm moving. That's all."

Darya drew her eyebrows together. She understood her aunt's words. She just didn't understand what they meant.

"I've found a garage apartment. It's charming and

I love it. And Vera and I shouldn't live here forever, should we?"

"Is Aunt Vera going with you?"

"No!" Aunt Elena exclaimed. She blushed. "I mean . . . *no*. Your aunt and I could benefit from our own space, don't you think?"

Darya didn't know *what* she thought.

"My new apartment is just outside of Old Town. Two minutes by car, twenty if you walk, so you can come see me anytime."

"But you live here," Darya said. "You've always lived here."

"Well, no." Aunt Elena slipped her hands under her thighs. "Before your mom left, I lived near the community college. I taught American literature. Did you know that?" She took a breath. "But now that Klara's back in town, it seems to me that we should start . . . making a space for her. A clean slate. Slowly, of course."

"But she'll come here, right? That's what you mean?" Darya heard herself say. Her words seemed to float up and out of her before evaporating in the harsh light of her room.

"She's not sure she's ready. And the motel she's in—it's not the nicest. You might as well know."

"So what are you saying, that she's going to stop living in the motel and live with you? In a garage apartment?"

Aunt Elena touched Darya's knee. "I know this is hard, Darya. It's hard for all of us."

Darya felt herself retreating inward. The world, for its part, moved steadily away from her, as if pulled by a giant rubber band.

"Are you going to tell Papa?"

Aunt Elena's eyes slid away.

"You aren't going to tell *Papa*? How can you not tell Papa?!"

"That's really your mom's decision. I know it's hard, I do—"

"I wish you'd stop saying that."

"But it is. It just *is*, sweetheart." Her voice came from far away. "Klara's had a rough time of it. Not always, but when she was your age, something happened. Something I keep trying to grab hold of . . ."

There was a stain on Darya's carpet. How interesting. A dull brownish-gray stain shaped like a comma, but bigger.

"It was because of her Wishing Day," Aunt Elena said. "You can relate to that, can't you? Since your own is coming up?"

"What does that have to do with anything?"

"When Klara was thirteen, she made a wish. Only, it went wrong."

The world came rushing back. "I know. Natasha told me. About how Papa had a little sister, and her name was Emily, and Mama 'wished' her away."

Aunt Elena studied her. "Listen to me, Darya. It's important. You didn't choose to be born into this family. I know that. Although we're very lucky to have you—and I hope you feel lucky to have us."

"I do."

"And I hope you feel lucky to have your mom, even though she left."

Darya fidgeted. "I *do*."

"The thing is, I think Klara left because she felt lost. But I'm afraid she might have come home lost, too."

Darya drew her knees up to her body and hugged her shins.

"Don't give up on her," Aunt Elena said. "That's all I'm saying."

"How have I given up on her? How could I have? I haven't even seen her!"

"I know, I know. *Shhh.*"

"Are you mad at me because of the Emily thing?"

"I'm not *mad*, Darya. Did I say I was mad?"

"And anyway, I'm not saying I blame Mama for telling that story, because maybe she does believe it. Just, I don't, because . . . you know."

Aunt Elena raised her eyebrows.

"I'm thirteen, Aunt Elena. Also, I'm *me*. Not Ava, not Natasha, but me. I believe in lots of stuff, but I'm not sure I believe in magic."

"Ah," Aunt Elena said. "The thing is, I'm not sure that matters."

"Then what does?"

Aunt Elena looked wistful. "Whether the magic believes in you."

# CHAPTER TWELVE

*Finally* it was Saturday!

Darya got up at the crack of dawn to help Papa and Ava load Papa's pickup with finished lutes. The sky was a fiery orange, without a hint of pink or purple. The lutes gleamed in the light, and Darya thought of alchemy: soft wood turned into softer gold.

Papa had on jeans and one of his nicer flannel shirts. Ava was wearing overalls, which she could pull off because she was Ava. Her hair was in two thick braids, and she'd gone so far as to stick a long blade of grass into one of them. She was playing the role of country bumpkin on purpose, maybe with the thought that it might help with sales, or maybe just because it was fun. Or maybe Ava was distracting herself from the news about Mama the same way Darya had tried to do?

Darya liked the "fun" idea better. She wanted Ava to have fun, and she felt guilty about going behind her back to see Mama. She certainly wouldn't be up this early if not for her guilt, which made her wonder: Where was Natasha?

Well, Natasha was sleeping in, obviously. Which led to a new question: How was she *able* to sleep in? Did Natasha *not* feel guilty?

Ava hopped out of the bed of the pickup truck, babbling about the craft festival she and Papa would be heading for. It was two towns over, and it was called the Fall Leaves Fest. There'd be cider and popcorn and face-painting, and was Darya positive she didn't want to come?

"A hundred percent," Darya said. "But will you bring me a caramel apple? With chocolate and peanuts on top. *Not* walnuts."

"I'll try," Ava said.

"If there aren't any with peanuts, then just caramel and chocolate. But not white chocolate, because white chocolate is a scam."

"I'll try," Ava said, climbing into the truck's front seat.

"No, you *will*, because if you don't, Papa will leave you behind. Right, Papa?"

Papa glanced up from the mileage log he'd been flipping through. "What's that?"

"Ava has to bring me a caramel apple or you'll disown her. Right?"

Ava giggled. Papa frowned.

"Disown her?" he said. "Why would I disown Ava?"

"You wouldn't. I was joking."

Papa closed his small black notebook and put it in his back pocket. "I don't understand."

Darya felt her insides lurch.

"Papa, it was a joke."

"How is it a joke, when I've lost so much already?" Papa said. He stared at Ava, and his pupils dilated. "I would *never* disown you, Emily. Never."

Ava went pale. She cast a look at Darya, who felt as if she were coming loose from her body.

"Papa, I know that," Darya said. "I was just . . . I didn't mean . . ."

Papa gazed at the sky, which was now the bleached blue of a work shirt washed many times over. Darya sought to see what he saw, and tiny shimmers of light pricked her eyes.

Then, in a flash, Darya saw through to another world, and in that world she saw a ghost of a girl who looked like Ava, though the dress the girl wore was out of style.

Papa climbed into the truck and turned the key. After two false starts, the motor caught, and the real world came back to life.

Ava closed her door and rolled down the window. "Bye! Have a good day!"

"You too," Darya replied. "Sell lots of lutes!"

"That's the plan," Papa said. "And we'll bring you a caramel apple if they have any, only not with walnuts because walnuts make your tongue burn."

Darya's smile slipped. Walnuts *did* make her tongue burn, but how did Papa know that? She'd told people she didn't *like* walnuts. That was all.

"It runs in the family," Papa said. "We'll see you this evening."

He drove off, kicking up rocks from the dirt driveway.

⌒

The motel where Mama was staying was worse than Darya had imagined. From the outside, at any rate. It was on the far edge of Willow Hill, dropped into a plot of dry earth and stub grass with nothing nearby but a lonesome gas station. Its courtyard once boasted a pool, but the pool had gone dry long ago. Now it was a concrete pit, run through with cracks and filled with grit and sticks and trash.

There were eight units in the hotel, built in the shape of a U.

"Mama's in number seven," Natasha said, coming to a stop when they were several yards away from the building.

Darya's eyes scanned the doors and rested on the second-to-last. The 7 hung askew, painted a dull red. The door itself was white, or had once been. Now it was weathered and gray.

"It's kind of depressing," Natasha said. "I know."

All Darya cared about was Mama, who was practically close enough to touch. The almost-there-ness of it all scared her, but her excitement was stronger than her fear.

*Mama*, not twenty feet away.

She smoothed down her hair and tried to calm her galloping heart—and then she just gave herself over to it. She hastened her pace and rapped on Mama's door so hard her knuckles stung.

"Mama?" she called. "Mama, it's me. Darya!"

She caught the flutter of curtains and a glimpse of pale skin. She heard a deadbolt slide free, and the door opened. Everything vanished except the woman before her.

Dark hair. Red lipstick. Anxious brown eyes that widened, then welled with tears as Darya flung herself into Mama's arms, gasping with the rightness of it.

She was four years old again, and also a teenager. Mama was *Mama* again, always and forever, and if she was different in any way, Darya chose not to notice, because now was a hugging and crying time. A laughing time, too. Great hiccupy laughs, because of how Darya's tears mixed with Mama's, making everything salty and gross and warm and lovely.

It was several minutes before they released each other. Even then, Mama kept hold of Darya's hands.

"Darya," she said. Her voice sounded deeper than Darya remembered. Huskier. Although it had been *so long* since Darya had spoken with her that she was probably just remembering wrong. Memories were like that. Tricky.

"You're so beautiful," Mama went on. She caught a lock of Darya's hair and pulled the curl through her fingers. She smiled. "You're so *big*."

Darya smiled back, her smile pushing all the way to the sides of her face.

Mama craned her neck to peer past Darya. "Natasha? Come on in."

Natasha squeezed in. It was a tight fit with all three of them wedged within the door frame.

Darya laughed, and Natasha said, "Hi, Mama," and gave her a quick kiss. She moved to a brown and ugly sofa wedged by the room's radiator and dropped down.

"Yes, have a seat, absolutely," Mama said, squeezing Darya's hands and then releasing them. "I'll . . . get us some lemonade. If we have any, which we probably don't." She punctuated her words with gestures, and both her speech and her mannerisms seemed wound up.

It was normal that there *were* differences, she supposed. It had been years, after all.

Mama strode toward the room's minibar, and Darya sat down beside Natasha. The smell of cigarette smoke wafted from the cushions.

"Nope, no lemonade," Mama said, closing the minibar's door. A key dangled from its lock, which struck Darya as odd. The minibar was in Mama's room, which Mama was paying for, so why the lock? Especially since the key was right there!

Mama came over to Darya and Natasha. She sat on the bed, which faced the sofa. She drew her eyebrows together, hopped up again, and returned with a wad of tissues, half of which she handed to Darya. The other tissues she used herself, blowing her nose and dabbing at her eyes.

"We're a bit of a mess, aren't we?" she said.

Darya blew her nose, and Mama looked delighted.

"You still do that!" she said.

"Do what?"

"Always," Natasha told Mama. "She doesn't know how to blow it any other way."

*Oh*, Darya thought. *The honking-ness of it.* There was a time when it embarrassed her, but she knew no other way.

"Once I tripped when you blew your nose," Mama confided, her eyes dancing. "I was walking up the stairs—you were downstairs making paper dolls—we were making them together, but we needed a better pair of scissors—and, *honk!*"

Darya giggled. "And you tripped?"

"Not with the scissors, I hope," Natasha said.

"Not with the scissors," Mama said. "And yes, I tripped right in the middle of the staircase. My little girl, my beautiful, perfect, little girl—*honk!*"

Darya was thrilled. A big sister teasing her younger sister, and their mother playing along. It was what she'd yearned for, and *here it was*. Something opened behind her ribs, and her lungs felt fragile, like wings.

She looked around the room, trying to find something to admire. Her gaze fell on a blue-and-purple quilt, made from dozens of circles, all sewn together. "Hey, I remember that! Aunt Elena made it! It used to live on the green sofa by the fireplace!"

Mama's smile dimmed. Then it grew bright again. "Aunt Elena *did* make it. Do you remember what it's called?"

"I do," Natasha rushed to say. "It's a yo-yo quilt."

"That's right," Mama said. "Darya, you helped make it. Do you remember?"

"What about me?" asked Natasha. "Did *I* help?"

Darya tried her best to ignore Natasha. She looked deep into Mama's eyes and pulled the details free. "We cut circles out of old scraps," she said. "We sat in front of the—"

She broke off. *No, don't mention the fireplace, or the sofa, or anything from home.*

"It was snowing outside. We cut circles out of whatever fabric we could find. Then we sewed a row of stitches around each circle and cinched the thread tight, which is why they're fluffy instead of flat. We made tiny, baby pouches, kind of."

"Yes, exactly!" Mama exclaimed, and Darya glowed. "Papa and I were dazzled by how clever you were. Mazes, puzzles, yo-yo quilts. You could do anything you set your mind to, Darya."

"I was clever, too," Natasha pestered. "Wasn't I?"

"Or course," Mama said, though she kept her focus on Darya. "You learned to read before you were three, you know. And that memory of yours! Nothing slipped by you."

"Nothing?"

"Nothing."

Natasha laughed, but it was obviously fake. "Omigosh, Darya. Quit fishing for compliments!"

"Natasha," Mama chided.

"Mama, I'm so glad you're back!" Darya said impulsively. "When are you going to tell Papa? I know about Aunt Elena's apartment or whatever. I know you're going to live with her for a while. But how long?"

Mama's expression changed. *Mama* changed. It was as if she grew harder and more brittle, and Natasha shot Darya a look.

"What?" she said. "I'm just asking."

"It's complicated," Mama said. "I'm not ready."

*Complicated, complicated, complicated*, Darya thought. *Hard, hard, hard.*

"What do you mean?" she said.

"I mean it would be a bad idea for me to go home."

"Um, okay, only . . ." She gulped. "I'm not trying to be rude, but why? I don't understand."

Mama stared at her. "Of course you don't. You don't have to *understand* things for them to *be*."

Darya recoiled.

"I tried to explain," Natasha said. "Only Darya doesn't believe in Emily. She thinks it's all made up."

Mama shook her head with fast, hard movements. She patted her shirt pocket and the back pockets of her jeans. She pressed her lips together, then said, "I need a cigarette."

Darya turned to Natasha. She was mad at her, and she knew Natasha was mad back, but they were sisters. "Mama *smokes*?" she mouthed.

"Sometimes," Natasha responded. "But *shhh*." Only instead of making an actual *shhh* sound, she put her finger to her lips.

"Well," Mama said. "Emily." She gave a sharp laugh. "You don't have to believe in Emily, Darya. Some people don't believe in souls. Some people don't believe in evolution. Some people don't believe in aliens!"

Mama was speaking faster and faster. Darya didn't like it. And . . . aliens?

"When someone unpicks the stitches that hold your life together, *then*. *Then* you'll see," Mama said. She stood and paced the length of the room. "I hope that never happens. But are you under the impression that we get to choose?"

"Mama, calm down, please," Natasha said nervously.

Mama jabbed her finger at them. Natasha and Darya jumped. Then Mama made a strange transformation, stretching her face into someone else's and adopting that someone else's voice.

"Calm *downnnn*, ma'am. Calm *downnnn*," she said in an accent that was maybe . . . Jamaican? That was Darya's best guess, because of the lilting syllables and elongated vowels.

It reminded her of Sebastian from *The Little Mermaid*, but Sebastian was funny. Mama was freaking Darya out.

"You need to re-*laaax*," Mama said. "Can you do that, or shall I ring for Dr. Feinstein?"

Darya looked at Natasha with eyes that said, *Dr. Feinstein?*

Natasha gave the quickest shake of her head. *Not now.*

Mama snorted. Accent abandoned, she said, "Pop a pill, all will be well. But girls, hear me when I say this: *It doesn't work like that.*"

"We know, Mama," Natasha said. "We believe you."

"How can you be calm when you know—you *know*—the truth inside you? And you *tell* them, but do they listen? If you weren't crazy already, it would make you crazy, you better believe that."

She patted her shirt pocket again and made a sound of frustration. "There was a young man. A young black man named Alan. I'd say it doesn't matter, the fact that he was black, but . . ." She splayed her hands, palms up. "*Well.* People judge, don't they?"

"What young man?" Darya asked. "Do we know him?"

"One morning Alan woke up, and he knew someone was after him." She thumped her chest with her fist. "He knew in his heart that before the day ended, he would be shot. He also knew he wasn't thinking straight, because that happens. Two opposing thoughts can live right next to each other in your brain—it happens all the time."

"So Alan . . ."

"It was on the radio! Listen for yourself if you don't believe me!"

"Mama," Darya pleaded. She'd hoped that with Mama back, everything would fall together the way it was supposed to. All the missingness and pain and confusion would be taken out of her hands. Instead, anguish coursed through her, hot as melted wax.

"He went to the hospital. He drove himself there. Drove straight into the building, because the delusions had gotten worse. He tried to explain. He told the doctors, the nurses—he told them everything! And do you know what happened?"

Nothing good, Darya was sure. She wanted to go home.

"'Calm down,' they told him. 'Relax!' And when he wouldn't put the hospital gown on, the nurse called for security, and a rent-a-cop came to Alan's room *and shot him.*"

Mama skewered them with her gaze. Then she laughed bitterly. "So what do you make of that, girls? He knew he was delusional . . . and yet look what happened. At the end of the day, who knows where the truth lies?"

The room filled with silence.

Darya was afraid she might cry again, but not the good kind of crying.

Natasha bowed her head.

Mama drooped, too. No one looked at anyone.

"I think maybe I'll go home," Darya managed to say. Her throat felt terribly clogged with formality.

"Oh, darling, no," Mama said. "Oh, baby." She reached forward and stroked Darya's cheek, and she was Mama again. But the other Mama, was she Mama, too?

Darya's lower lip trembled, and Mama was up and hugging her before Darya could protest.

"Oh, sweet girl, I'm so sorry," Mama said, disarmed by regret. Her words were soft. *She* was soft, where before she'd been hard. "It's too much. *I'm* too much. I have . . . I have mood swings, darling Darya. It's complicated. I know it is. But it's not for you to worry about, and I'm sorry. I'm sorry, I'm sorry, I'm sorry."

She rocked Darya in her arms, and Darya filled with doubt. Beautiful, unexpected doubt, which turned into a seed of hope, which blossomed like a sunflower.

Of course Mama's life was complicated. There was no way Darya could know the ins and outs of it all.

"It's all right," she said.

Mama drew back and peered at Darya. "You know what? Let's take a walk, just the two of us. Natasha's had time to absorb all this—we've had so much time together, haven't we, Natasha? And so much more to come. But Natasha, sweetheart, would you mind terribly if I stole Darya away for a bit?"

Twin spots of color rose on Natasha's cheeks. "No, that's totally fine."

Mama smiled. She stroked Darya's cheek, and then Natasha's. "Such good girls."

"Ava, too," Darya said.

A cloud passed over Mama's face, but she was quick to make it disperse. "Of course Ava, too. But Natasha, please don't feel like I'm kicking you out. *We'll* leave. We'll take a walk, Darya and I, and you stay as long as you'd like."

"I'll just go on home," Natasha said. "I've got homework to do, anyway. Darya, can you find your way back?"

"I think I can manage," Darya said. Mama's motel was hardly in the heart of Willow Hill, but Willow Hill was hardly a booming metropolis. "We *did* leave a trail of breadcrumbs, didn't we?"

Mama inhaled sharply.

"She's kidding," Natasha said.

"Are you?" Mama asked Darya.

"Mama. Of course."

"You girls," Mama said, forcing a laugh.

*She's struggling too,* Darya reminded herself. *It is complicated.*

"A walk sounds good," Darya said. "Moving around always helps, you know?"

Mama loosened with relief, and Darya felt proud.

"I'll be home before it gets late," she told Natasha. "If anyone asks where I am . . . well, they won't. But tell them whatever you want."

Truth, with a capital *T*, was elusive. But time with Mama—time *alone* with Mama . . .

She knew she might not get the answers she craved.

She didn't care.

She just wanted her mother, and even the smallest breadcrumbs felt like a feast.

# CHAPTER THIRTEEN

Mama walked at a fast clip, a ball cap pulled low over her face and her thumbs hooked through the belt loops of her jeans. They headed away from town, because Mama didn't want to risk seeing anyone.

"I'm not ready yet," she said. "I'm just not." She shot a sideways glance at Darya. "Do you understand?"

*Yes . . . and no*, Darya thought. She understood the urge to hide. She understood that sharing yourself with others, *revealing* yourself to others, was scary.

On the other hand, Mama was moving into a garage apartment with Aunt Elena soon. How would she hide then? Because the apartment wasn't all that far from their house, according to Aunt Elena. That meant they'd be in town. There'd be people who could see and hear and notice, people who would love to spread the news that Klara Blok had returned from the dead.

What if Papa found out about Mama's return from Ms. McKinley? Or from Barney, the man-child who bagged groceries at Beaver's Market? Barney was sweet but dull-witted. If Barney saw Mama, he wouldn't think twice about mentioning her to Papa.

Nor should he, really. *Anyone* who saw Mama would assume Papa knew she was back. He was her husband. They were married. So how, exactly, was Mama planning on living in this garage apartment while never showing her face?

They walked without speaking until they reached the lonely gas station that was the stepbrother of the lonely motel. There was a single pump, but no cars being refueled. Several yards away stood a ramshackle building with posters on the windows advertising Coke products, a two-for-one offer on toilet paper, and access to an ATM for all paying customers. Only there were no customers that Darya could see.

When she squinted, she made out a cash register

behind a counter crammed with impulse-buy items. She saw no one manning the register. Maybe he or she was in the bathroom.

Mama dug in her front pocket and pulled out a ten-dollar bill. "Baby, pop inside and buy me a package of Camels, will you?"

Darya stared at her.

Mama waggled the bill, then made a sound of impatience when Darya didn't take it.

"Mama . . . I'm thirteen," Darya said.

"Of course you are! That's why I asked Natasha to tell you about me, goose. I missed her thirteenth birthday—I wasn't about to miss yours!"

*But . . . you did,* Darya thought. *You did miss my birthday, and because of you, Aunt Elena missed it too.*

She shook her head. "Yeah, but I'm not allowed, I'm pretty sure."

"To buy your mother cigarettes?" Mama said, her voice hiking in disbelief. "Old Ned's not going to care." She wiggled the bill again. "Just . . . please. It's a nasty habit. I'm going to quit. But I want to talk to you, Darya. Really *talk* to you, mother to daughter, because there's so much to get caught up on." She barked a laugh. "Only, my nerves! I'm shaking, see?!"

*Why can't you do it yourself?* Darya wanted to ask.

But Mama's fingers *were* trembling. She had fine lines spraying out from the corners of her eyes, worry lines, but they grew smoother when Darya shrugged and took the money.

"Menthols, please. Or better yet, Turkish Gold, but no one has Turkish Gold anymore." She pushed at her hair. "Menthols. Menthols will be great. And if you want a pack of gum, you can buy that, too."

She smiled tightly. *Go on, then,* her expression said, so Darya walked stiffly into the gas station and approached the dusty counter.

"Hello?" she called, scanning the store. "Um . . . I need to buy cigarettes. For my mom. Is anyone—"

"Get what you need. Leave the money on the counter," said a grouchy male voice from somewhere in the vicinity of the cold drinks. Old Ned, Darya supposed.

"Are you sure?" Darya said. Even if it was legal for her to purchase cigarettes—and she knew it wasn't—she surely wasn't supposed to go behind the counter and get them herself.

"If you want them, buy them. If you don't, leave."

Darya started to protest, then closed her mouth. Mama wanted cigarettes. Not cool, but fine. Whatever.

If Old Ned had no interest in a face-to-face exchange, all the better.

She marched behind the counter and stretched high to pull a pack of Camel Menthols from the shelf. She circled back, slapped down the ten-dollar bill, and left. The bell on the door jangled as it shut behind her.

"Here," she said, thrusting the Camels at Mama.

Mama tore open the cellophane and shook a cigarette from the pack. She lit it and sucked at it greedily, closing her eyes as she blew out a long plume of smoke.

Darya coughed, and Mama laughed, which hurt Darya's feelings.

"Oh, baby, I'm sorry," Mama said. "So many sorries. So many things to apologize for! But *oh*, this is good. Thank you, sweet Darya. This hits the spot."

After three more long drags, Mama crushed the cigarette out and tossed it into the trash. She began walking again, this time with a jauntier stride. Darya fell in beside her.

"I saw a field of sunflowers once," Mama said. "Two summers ago? Maybe three? They were so lovely. They made me think of you." She glanced at Darya. "There was a path that cut through the field. A winding dirt path, and two big trees where the path topped a hill. Beyond the hill, I could no longer see it. Do you know what it made me think of?"

"What?"

When Mama smiled, her whole face lit up. "Possibilities. Fresh starts. Accepting the fact that life is a journey, you know?" She fisted her hands and pulled them in. "But we can grab hold of it. That's up to us. The path is there, yes, but *we* get to decide whether to follow it, and for how long, or if we want to veer off altogether. Don't you think?"

"Um, sure?"

Mama's expression was warm and kind and . . . *motherly*, as if she were pleased with Darya despite Darya's totally lame reply. She seemed at ease, and glad to have Darya all to herself, and Darya figured the nicotine had worked its magic.

*Don't judge*, Darya told herself. But she swore that she would never start smoking, never in a million years.

"Do you still like flowers?" Mama asked.

"I do. I love them."

"So do I, always and forever." Mama's gait was loose now, more of a stroll than a stride. "And art? Are you still interested in art?"

"Um, yeah, I guess." She *was* interested in art. She just wasn't any good at it. "I'm taking art as my

146

elective. My friend, Tally? She's new. She lives with a foster family. Well, foster parents. I don't know if there are other kids."

She also didn't know where this word vomit was coming from. She told herself to *put a lid on it, butter-cup*, yet the words kept spewing out. "But she's *really* good at art. Tally. Like, will probably end up in the Louvre good."

Mama laughed happily. It wasn't easy to walk, talk, and have eye contact at the same time, but Mama was making a good go of it, peppering Darya with smiles and quick, sparkly glances.

"That's fantastic," she said. "You and Sally can end up in the Louvre together! How about that?"

"Um, yeah," Darya said. "Only, it's Tally, not Sally."

The sky was a dazzling, optimistic blue. The sun warmed her skin. *It takes time for two people to get reacquainted*, she reminded herself.

Mama headed off the road. "Let's sit," she said, making a beeline for a leafy magnolia tree. "Is this good?" She dropped to the ground and patted the spot beside her.

Darya lowered herself to the grass.

"You must have realized I came back for a reason," Mama said.

Darya's stomach clenched. She hadn't, really. Not when Mama put it like that.

"It's *you*, Darya. I came back because of you."

"*Me?*"

"But you can't tell the others, especially your sisters."

A sliver of sunlight cut through the shadows and dappled Mama's features, making her look asymmetrical. It reminded Darya of that Picasso painting—Picasso? Or van Gogh?—in which a woman's face appeared to have been split apart and reassembled, only not very neatly.

Mama's smile flashed, half dark and half light. "We're connected, you and I. We're all connected, really—whether we want to be or not."

"I guess so."

"Oh, don't guess. *Know.*"

Darya balled her hands into fists, which she hid in her lap.

"The threads of your life are woven into the fabric of mine, and vice versa," Mama said. "That's the way it is with families! You get that, right?" She leaned in and loaded each word with weight. "Nobody. Exists. Alone."

Darya wet her lips. "I . . . yeah. I can see that."

"When I think of Emily—and believe me, I think of Emily all the time—I try to imagine what she'd be like as an adult. As a woman. My age."

*But I don't believe in Emily*, Darya said silently. *Or, I don't* want *to. Can't we change the subject?*

"I will never forget her," Mama said. Her gaze locked on Darya as if what she was telling her was the most important thing she'd told anyone, ever. "I will never leave Emily again. I can't. And Emily will never leave me."

Shards of sadness pierced Darya's heart, because whatever the truth was—whatever *Mama's* truth was, whatever Mama *thought* it was—it was eating her up. At the same time, Darya was frightened. The brightness of Mama's eyes pinned her down, making her think of butterflies pinned to one of those awful display boards.

Dead butterflies. Dead Emily.

There were forces at work here bigger than anything Darya had conceived of before now. Worse, Darya wasn't sure if the forces wanted a good outcome or a bad outcome, or if "good" and "bad" came into play at all.

Mama slapped her breastbone. She did it again. "There's such a hole inside me! If I don't fill it, I'll die. I'll *die*!"

"Mama. Shhh. It's fine, everything's fine." Darya glanced around, but there was no one in sight. She had Mama all to herself, just as she'd wanted.

Mama inhaled sharply, then exhaled with just as much force. She closed her eyes and touched her fingertips to her eyebrows, and Darya thought of a little kid counting quietly in her head in an attempt to calm down. *Three, two, one—one, two, three. What the heck is bothering me?*

"You're right," Mama said. "I'm sorry. I get . . . worked up." *Four, five, six, seven, eight, nine, later I'll have a bottle of wine.*

Not that Mama drank wine, not to Darya's knowledge.

Then again, Darya's knowledge was pretty sparse.

What *did* Darya know about her mother?

Mama's lips curved up. It wasn't exactly a smile, but Darya did her best to mirror it back.

"The thing is . . ." Mama breathed in and out. She smiled again. "*The thing is*, I've figured it out."

"Figured what out?"

"At first I thought Natasha, maybe, but no. That

150

ship has already sailed." She threw out her hands. "What can you do, right?"

"Hey, how about we go back to the motel?" Darya said. "If Natasha's still there, we don't want her to be stuck waiting for us."

"Your sister's not waiting for us. Your sister's gone."

Darya felt a coldness creep over her.

"Natasha's Wishing Day is a thing of the past, but not yours," Mama said.

"I don't—"

"It's so simple. Don't you see?" She took Darya by the shoulders. "You have to wish Emily back."

# CHAPTER FOURTEEN

On the outside, Darya suspected that she looked the same as she had a moment before. But on the inside, everything had changed. It was as if . . . as if she'd turned in on herself. She'd fallen into a hole—not Mama's hole, but her own—and she was still falling.

Things didn't make sense.

There was nothing to grab hold of.

She'd heard of this sort of thing, how people floated free of their bodies when life became too much. "It was like I was looking down at myself," a girl being interviewed on television might say after experiencing something horrible. She'd frown prettily, and the television reporter would knit her eyebrows and gesture for the girl to go on.

The girl would hesitate for a beat. She'd swallow, maybe, then say, "I could see what I was doing. I could hear the words coming out of my mouth! But I wasn't there. I'd gone someplace safe until the awfulness was over."

People watching from their own safe houses would murmur and make sympathetic sounds as they spooned mac and cheese into their mouths or swigged Coke from a red-and-white can that said *Legend* or *Star* or *BFF*.

*Poor girl*, they'd think.

*Poor me*, Darya thought.

Mama was still talking. She was still holding Darya's shoulders, her fingers digging into the skin on either side of her shoulder blades.

Darya twisted away. "You're hurting me!" she cried. "Stop!"

Mama released Darya. A dazed look clouded her eyes. After a moment, her features sharpened and her pupils refocused.

"So you understand what to do? That's all that matters. It's all sorted out, then!"

Darya's head ached. She pushed herself up and got

her feet to do what she needed them to do. Right foot, forward. Left foot, forward.

She heard scrabbling sounds as Mama darted to catch up.

"Are you going back to the motel?" she said. "Do you want some tea? Or how about a Fanta Grape? You used to love Fanta Grape. Do you still? You loved the bubbles and that horrible purple color. I'd serve it to you in a champagne flute, and you'd hold it up to the sunlight. 'Fairy juice, Mama!' you'd say. 'It's what the fairies drink, and I do too!'"

Mama laughed.

Darya wanted to swat her, and the impulse scared her. She'd never wanted to swat anyone in her life, not for real. Not with such a twisty-turvy coiled-up feeling rising so rapidly inside her.

"That wasn't me, that was Ava," she said shortly.

Mama faltered. "It was? Are you sure?"

No, Darya wasn't sure. At age four, Ava was unlikely to have mused charmingly about fairies while sipping soda from a champagne flute. Darya doubted that she would have, either. Even though she was so smart! So clever! Reading when she was three, solving riddles when she was four!

And Natasha? Not a fairy-juice sort of girl.

"I'm sure," she said curtly.

The sun, which had caressed her earlier in the day, beat mercilessly against her fair skin. *More freckles!* she thought. *Lucky me!*

"Darya, you're acting strange," Mama said.

"Am I? I'm sorry."

"What's wrong, sweetheart?"

*Are you kidding me?* Darya wanted to say. *Are you fricking kidding me?!* She pressed her lips together and walked faster, *not* toward Mama's motel, but not home, either.

*Someplace safe until the awfulness was over.* But where was that, and when would the awfulness be over? Tears burned at her eyes, stinging with a confusion that had nowhere to land.

"You can't bring back a dead person," she said.

"Ex*cuse* me?" Mama said.

A lump grew in Darya's throat. Stupid tears spilled out, and she swiped at them with the back of her hand.

"I *said*, excuse me?" Mama repeated. "*You* can't bring back anyone. You're absolutely right about that. But I didn't ask you to, did I?"

Whirling around, Darya cried, "How can you say

155

that? That's *exactly* what you asked me to do!"

"A wish. Is not. *You*," Mama said.

A breeze rose from nowhere, only it was stronger than a breeze. It whipped Darya's red curls around her face.

"You can *make* the wish," Mama said. She jabbed her finger at Darya. "But the wish"—jab—"is"—jab— "the wish. Got it?"

"No, I don't!"

"And who said anything about Emily being dead? Did I say Emily was dead? No, I did not."

"Um, I'm pretty sure you did!"

Mama sighed, and Darya's breath got stuck in her chest. Usually when someone sighed, it made the person appear smaller. Mama's sigh made her grow larger.

"There are *mysteries* in this world," Mama said. A muscle jumped in her jaw. "I told you that, Darya. I told you! And just because we can't understand something, or explain it—"

"But Mama!" Darya said. "Okay, just . . . *if*. If Emily is, or was, or—*no*! Let me finish!"

Mama, who'd taken a step forward, lifted her palms as if in surrender. Her eyes flashed, but she stayed where she was.

"If Emily . . . used to be here, but now she isn't . . ." Darya felt like she had yellow jackets buzzing around in her head. "Wouldn't bringing her back change the whole past?"

The sun dipped behind gray clouds. Darya caught the metallic scent of soon-to-come rain.

"Like, say Emily just popped back into existence," she went on. "Wouldn't that change the lives of every person who ever . . . came in contact with her? What if you didn't marry Papa? What if you did, but on a different day, because Emily thought a spring wedding would be lovely or whatever?"

"We did have a spring wedding," Mama said. "Do you know why? Because I knew that's what Emily would have wanted."

"But if it was different *at all*, there might not have been *us*," Darya said, meaning herself and her sisters. "If today, or on my Wishing Day, or whenever, I wish for something that changes the past, and my wish comes *true* . . ."

Darya imagined a piece of cloth laid flat, but with a wrinkle at the far left side. If left alone, then fine. There'd be a piece of cloth with a wrinkle in it. But if the wrinkle was smoothed out, it would have to be pushed from the left side all the way to the right side, until *poof*! With the flutter of air, the fabric would lie flat. Only, it would lie flat in a whole new way.

Not that Darya *believed* in any of this.

Mainly.

But what if she did? Anyone who knew anything knew that messing with the past was asking for trouble. The fact that Mama didn't seem to see that—or if she did, that she didn't seem to care—made Darya feel very small and very sad.

"Sometimes things aren't true, but should have been," Mama said.

Darya gazed at Mama, attempting to discern some sort of meaning in her cryptic remark.

"I *need* you to do this for me," Mama said. "I *need* you to help bring Emily back."

Darya had assumed that with Mama back, things would be better. That Mama would *make* them better. That she'd step back into their lives, and the transition would be hard, but she'd do what mothers were supposed to do. She'd say to her daughters, "Here, let me fix this for you. Let me take this weight off your shoulders. Let me, let me, let *me*."

But Mama's return had made things worse, not better. Instead of happiness and hugs and warm apple pies, she'd brought new troubles to the Blok family. New secrets. Bad secrets.

A raindrop splashed onto Darya, then another. It started to drizzle, and through the blur of the raindrops, Darya appraised Mama once more.

Her hair was thick and shiny, and her eyes held hints of her long-ago warmth, and Darya did kind of like how Mama wore jeans and a flannel shirt and a swipe of red lipstick. She looked tough, if worn down. If she got lost in the forest, Darya suspected, she'd find her way out. In fact, hadn't she done precisely that, even if the forest hadn't been a literal forest?

Or maybe it had been. Who knew?

"I'm glad you're back," Darya told her. Hot tears spilled down her face, mixing with the cool rain. "I'm g-glad you're all right."

"Darya," Mama warned.

"But Emily's your problem, not mine. And I th-think you should talk to Papa. I think it's really awful that you haven't."

She spun on her heel and fled.

"Darya!" Mama called after her. "Darya, baby, please!"

Darya's sneakers slapped the ground. Her curls grew wet and heavy, clinging to her skin wherever they managed to latch on. Snot ran from her nose, and her chest heaved with sobs and the struggle to suck in air, and it was all Mama's fault because Mama hadn't saved Darya after all.

# CHAPTER FIFTEEN

*(before)*

Darya is wearing her favorite dress, the white one with tiny umbrellas floating down it like a million Mary Poppinses, just without Mary Poppins herself, or any other nanny.

Darya loves the movie of *Mary Poppins*. Natasha says there's books about her too, that Darya should read the books instead of watching the movie over and over, because books are better than movies.

But Darya loves the movie.

She especially loves Mary Poppins's friend, Bert, who is a chimney sweep. He talks funny and dances on rooftops, and Darya's favorite bit is when he hops on top of the tallest chimney of all—which is a *chimney* and has a *hole* going straight down it, a long black *deep* hole—and scissors his legs right over that hole. Crisscross, crisscross, and at the same time flapping his arms and singing the "Step in Time" song, which is the happiest song in the world, probably.

And yet, he *could* fall. Every time, Darya thinks about that, although she knows he won't.

Darya doesn't think Willow Hill has nannies or chimney sweeps, but today her preschool class is pretending they do. Miss Annie taught them three songs from *Mary Poppins*, and today is their performance. They won't be singing "Step in Time," but they will sing the other chimney sweep song, which is called "Chim Chim Cher-ee."

It's not a happy song, but Darya likes it anyway. She likes making big eyes and using a whisper voice for the scary-ish part, which she practices while Miss Annie goes around smoothing the girls' hair and telling the boys to be still.

"'When there's hardly no day nor hardly no night, there's things half in shadow and halfway in light,'" she sings under her breath.

It gives her the shivers. Delicious shivers, and she knows Mama will feel the same way.

"They're here! They're taking their seats!" Miss Annie tells the children, meaning the parents and grandparents who have arrived for the show. "Now remember, *eyes on me*. Let's show them how marvelous you are!"

The lights on the makeshift stage are bright and make Darya squint. Her tummy does a flip, and Mr. Evans starts up on the piano, and everyone sings "Chim Chim Cher-ee" just right, even Cyrus Conroy, who can't be counted on not to giggle.

Next they sing "Feed the Birds," which is beautiful and sad and has the word *tuppence* in it, which is fancy for two pennies. Darya's stomach starts to settle down, and she looks for Mama and Papa in the rows of folding chairs, even though she's not supposed to.

Finally, for their last act, they sing "A Spoonful of Sugar," and this song has dance moves in it. Easy ones, but still Darya has to concentrate. She gets every step right, and she remembers to "be expressive," which means pretending *to be* Jane (for the girls) or Michael (for the boys).

Jane and Michael are the children who need the nanny, because their parents don't have time for them. In this song, they have to clean up the nursery, which in Willow Hill would just be the den or the TV room or

163

just the kids' own bedroom. Cleaning up the nursery is a chore, but Mary Poppins makes it fun, and Darya acts all of this out with her gestures and expressions.

She's flushed with pride when the song ends and the audience claps and Miss Annie smiles and makes a *go on* motion, which means that yes, Darya and the others can scramble off the stage and run to find their parents.

She is swept up in a sea of grown-ups and fabric and strong perfume. She's pushed into a metal chair, and pain shoots through her hip. Maybe she'll have a bruise tomorrow. She likes bruises.

But where are Mama and Papa? They promised they'd be here. They promised especially *to be on time*, because when they're late, Darya gets a stomachache.

"Okay, Mama?" Darya had said this morning. She'd already eaten her oatmeal. It was the package kind, where each package makes one bowl and all Darya has to do is add hot water from the faucet. It wasn't as good as Mama's kind, but Mama was still in bed.

She'd shaken Mama's shoulder, and Mama had groaned from under the covers.

"The program starts at ten o'clock, but parents can

164

come at nine forty-five." She'd shaken her again. "Just say 'okay,' okay?"

"Yes, yes, okay," Mama had said, and she'd given Darya a sleepy kiss before telling her to break her leg, because that's what mothers were supposed to say before their daughters sang and danced on a stage.

Papa had given her a hug from his workshop. He'd promised they'd be on time, too.

So where are they?

"Darya! You were *won*derful!" Darya hears, and her insides slide all the way to her shoes even as she's pulled tight into Aunt Elena's embrace. "You were the cutest, yummiest, most fabulous spoonful of sugar ever. I am *so* proud of you!"

She doesn't tell Aunt Elena that she wasn't an actual spoonful of sugar.

She doesn't listen to why Mama couldn't make it, or why Papa had to stay with her.

She doesn't eat the snack that Cyrus's mom brought—a baggie of popcorn and a juice box for every kid in the class—and she doesn't say thank you to Cyrus's mom, either.

That afternoon, when she's back at home because half-day preschool is over, she sits in a sunny spot on the floor of the den. She practices not being there, even though she is. She doesn't turn to look when she hears Mama walk into the room. She doesn't lift her head when she sees Mama's bare feet in front of her. She tries to not even *see* Mama's feet.

*They're blobs*, she tells herself. *Just floaty potato blobs.* If she gazes past them, sort of, and lets her eyelids droop, they really and truly are.

Mama talks at her, with sorries and headaches and *sometimes it's just too hard, my sweet girl.*

"Okay," Darya tells the potato blobs.

"Aunt Elena said you were *won*derful," Mama says.

"Okay."

Mama sighs.

"Let's make up, Darya," she says. "Let's have a fresh start. Can we do that?"

Seconds tick by.

Mama squats all the way down and takes Darya's chin. "Can you look at me, at least?"

Darya does, reluctantly. She has so many feelings inside her that she doesn't know what to do, and she digs her fingernails into her palms.

Mama smiles, and a flare of hope lights up her

eyes. "I know, let's do a picture puzzle! Would you like that?"

Darya shakes her head. Everything's blurry because of *Can you look at me, at least?* And with everything blurry, a picture puzzle would be blurry as well, and Darya might get it wrong. Getting it wrong would be like falling off a cliff. That's how scary it feels.

"I don't have any paper," Darya says.

"We have paper," Mama says. "I can get some."

"I don't have a pencil."

"I'll get a pencil, too. Don't you worry."

Mama rises, and Darya's heart pounds.

"No, because my fingers hurt!" she says.

Mama pauses. Darya is afraid she's going to say, "I'll draw it, silly," but she doesn't. She just says, "My poor baby."

She lowers herself back to the floor. She sits all the way down and tucks her feet beneath her, and then she takes Darya's hands and rubs Darya's fingers. She doesn't mention the moon shapes dotting Darya's palms, although she traces them with the tip of her index finger.

"How about a different sort of puzzle?" she asks. "A new kind. Not a drawing kind, but a thinking kind.

A riddle. Would you like to try a riddle, my smart girl?"

Darya takes a breath, then blows the air from her puffed cheeks. "Is it hard?"

"Some are. Some aren't. Hard isn't necessarily bad, though."

"Then you should get out of bed in the morning!" Darya says. Immediately electricity shoots up and down her body. She did not mean those words! Or, maybe she did, but she didn't mean to *say* them!

Silence makes a storm cloud in the room.

Darya switches positions and draws her legs to her chest, holding them tight-tight-tight with wrapped-around arms.

"How do you make the number one disappear?" Mama asks.

"Huh?"

"That's the riddle. How do you make the number one disappear?"

"Is there a picture that goes with it?"

Mama shakes her head. She looks sad, and Darya wonders if this is her punishment. Making Mama sad makes Darya sad.

"You add a *g* and it's *gone*," Mama says.

Darya thinks about it. She does use a picture, but she makes it in her head, not on a piece of paper. *G* plus *one* equals . . . *ohhhh.*

She smiles. Mama smiles back.

"Okay, I have a riddle," Darya says. "How do you make sad disappear?"

"Hmm," Mama says. "You tell me."

"You add a *g* and an *l*, and . . ."

She stops.

Mama chuckles, which doesn't help. In fact, it makes her mad.

Mad, sad, glad.

They all have *ad*—but what do you *add* to get them?

"Hey," Mama says.

Darya meets Mama's eyes.

"I like your riddle. I think it's very clever, even if it doesn't quite work." She ruffles Darya's hair. "I'm sorry I laughed, but Darya?"

"What?"

"I wasn't laughing at you. And do you know what else?"

"What?"

"When things *don't* work, we just keep trying."

Darya can feel her chest go up and down. She already knows this. She *does* keep trying. Always.

But sometimes saying things out loud makes them

come true . . . and maybe Mama needs help? For herself?

"Okay," she says.

Mama pulls her into a hug, and her sad feelings and her mad feelings slip away.

For now, they are *g* plus *one*.

Gone.

# CHAPTER SIXTEEN

Darya didn't go back to see Mama at the motel, and she didn't visit her at Aunt Elena's charming garage apartment.

Autumn came on, and as the days grew shorter, Darya fell farther. She fell farther from Mama, and even the idea of Mama. She fell farther away from her sisters, her aunts, and Papa, too. She didn't choose to. It just happened. The farther she fell, the lonelier she grew.

Sometimes she thought about running away . . . but that would be ridiculous. Babyish. Mama-ish!

Sometimes, on the way to and from school when the dying leaves sighed from the trees, she softened and let the thought in: What if, eight years ago, *Mama* disappeared because of someone else's Wishing Day wish? It wasn't impossible, was it?

Or maybe it was, but maybe possible and impossible were adjectives without much meaning anymore.

Plus, she'd remember that Mama *chose* to leave. She walked away on her own two feet because she was so sad about Emily. Now she was back—hooray?—but she wanted Darya to make things better. Except life didn't work that way. Mama messed up, so Mama had to accept the consequences.

If there weren't any consequences, then why did anything matter?

Only . . . what if Darya was being so sullen and withdrawn because . . . oh, who knew? Because Neely from her math class made a wish that spiraled out of control? Maybe Neely, whom Darya didn't even talk to other than to compliment her outfit now and again, wished for a batch of cookies, and the cookies had poison in them—or something—and Darya ended up eating one, and voilà. Pouty Darya. Withdrawn Darya. "Darya"—cue dramatic movie preview voice—"falling from a tree."

Okay, not cookies, or Darya would have remembered eating one. Cafeteria Jell-O, then! Anything! Anything or nothing, because that was where the logic led her, and so *no*. No special allowances for Mama just because her wish went bad, if it even did.

Thinking about it made her head hurt, and she'd forgotten what it felt like to be happy, it seemed, and nobody even noticed. Or if they did, they certainly didn't ply her with cupcakes and soft words and *Oh, sweetie, everything's going to be all right*s.

"I guess I'll keep suffering silently," she told Tally in the art room, after filling her in on the basics. *Not* the part about her mother being back in Willow Hill. Just the most basic of the basics: that she was confused about her Wishing Day, and sad, and no one cared.

"But too bad for me, right?" she said.

Tally put down her pencil.

"I'll cry on the inside so that I don't bother my family," she continued, "because heaven forbid I *bother* anyone. They'll regret it when I wither away, though." She paused. "I'll wither quietly, of course."

"Of course," Tally said. "Just, help me out. Will you be suffering silently or withering quietly?"

"Both!" Darya said. "I'll suffer silently *while* withering quietly, and then . . . I don't know. I'll suffer and wither, and then I guess I'll die."

Tally studied her for a moment. Then she returned to her drawing. "Fine," she said.

"*Fine?* Did you just say *fine*?"

Tally's sketch was of a small girl sitting in the middle of a large sofa. With quick, sure strokes, she added shading to the girl's features. "We all will, won't we?"

"We all will what?"

"Die. Eventually."

"But . . ." Darya made an indignant sound. "That's not the point."

"You want me to feel sorry for you," Tally said, adding crosshatches to the worn part of the sofa. "That's the point, right? Only guess what? I don't."

"I never said you had to feel sorry for me," Darya argued, her cheeks growing hot.

"Didn't you?" Tally said.

*Not in those words*, Darya wanted to say.

Tally exhaled. She put down her pencil again and swiveled to face Darya straight on. "Listen. I am sorry you're suffering silently or whatever, but you're pretty lucky, Darya. In the big scheme, I mean."

"I am?"

"Um, *yes.* You have a family who *loves* you, Darya.

Do you know how awesome that is? Do you know how much I would give for that? Your mom's not in the picture. That sucks."

Darya wanted to correct her, but bit her tongue.

"Mine's not, either," Tally went on. "*Or* my dad."

"Where *is* he, your dad?" Yes, Darya was changing the subject, but she wanted to know.

"Gone," Tally said flatly. "He married my mom. She took his last name. Claimed she didn't *know* what her own last name was. Can you believe that?" She gave a short laugh. "Bet they had fun with that at the courthouse."

"Is that where they had the ceremony? At a court-house?"

"I kinda doubt there was a ceremony, but you're sweet—I guess—to think there might have been."

Darya's cheeks heated up.

"But, so, and then he left. I mean, first he got my mom pregnant, but he didn't stick around to meet me. Too bad, so sad, right?"

"Tally . . ."

"No. Please don't. Just admit that I've got a point. My mom's gone; your mom's gone. My dad's gone, but *yours isn't.*"

"Well . . ." Darya hedged. She imagined Papa in his workshop, his graying hair flopping over his lonely eyes.

"No, not, 'Well . . . ,'" Tally said. "You have a dad. He's here. He's physically present and part of your life. And he loves you, doesn't he?"

"Yes, but—"

"And your sisters! They're cool, Darya! Natasha's really nice every time I talk to her in the hall—"

"You've talked to Natasha in the hall? When?"

"And Ava is adorable. She's like a wind sprite or a . . . an elf. A cute elf, not a creepy one. And back to your Wishing Day, which is stressing you out. Think about it like this: At least you get a Wishing Day, so you better not even think about wasting it."

*Oh yeah*, Darya thought. Tally moved to Willow Hill after it was too late for her to have a Wishing Day of her own.

Tally narrowed her eyes. "Did Natasha's wishes really come true?"

Darya had a brain zap, a buzzing behind her skull that came and went and left her feeling dizzy. "Did they? I don't know. Who said that?"

Tally's gaze softened. She put her hand on Darya's forearm, and Darya flinched.

176

"People say your family's special," Tally said. "Not just Steph and Suki. Other people say that, too." She nodded, more to herself than to Darya. "Special in a good way."

"Ok-a-a-a-y."

"So don't stress out about your Wishing Day. Plan for it. Use it. If there's even a chance that your wishes'll come true . . ."

"Wait. Now you believe in the magic? At first you were so . . . you know. Skeptical."

Tally half laughed. "It *does* sound nuts, but just take advantage, you know? Don't throw something away just because you're mad about your sisters not"—she circled her hand through the air—"bringing you hot tea and those stupid warm washcloths scented with jasmine or whatever."

"Um, my sisters have never brought me warm washcloths scented with jasmine," Darya said. "*Or* hot tea."

"Idiots," Tally said.

"Ingrates!"

Tally smiled. After a second, Darya joined in.

"So . . . do what you can while you're still able," Tally said.

"Meaning?"

"Use your wishes. Use them *wisely*, like old ladies in fairy tales say. And then move on, and don't worry about it, because in the long run, everyone will forget anyway. Like you said."

"I said that? When?"

Tally shrugged. "You used different words, maybe. But yeah, eventually we're all going to die."

"Lovely," Darya said, slightly shaken. For one thing, it was much more satisfying to die when you weren't immediately forgotten. For another, Darya hadn't said that. Tally had.

She pulled her gaze away from her friend and stood up. She'd had enough of being comforted for the day.

*Darya.*

*Darya.*

*Darya.*

—MAMA, AGE THIRTY-FIVE

# CHAPTER SEVENTEEN

The weather grew cooler as September drifted into October. Darya's Wishing Day was getting closer. So was Halloween. Most people, Darya figured, cared more about Halloween.

But she'd been wrong about Natasha and Ava. They had noticed her melancholy. Natasha tried to broach the subject more than once, but Darya couldn't make the closed feeling around her heart go away. Natasha had continued to go visit Mama. She'd told Darya so. That meant Natasha was in league with Mama, which meant that Darya had lost her mother *and* her big sister. That was what it felt like.

She might as well throw in Aunt Elena as well, since Aunt Elena had been living in her charming garage apartment for nearly a month now. She hadn't invited everyone over yet because she was still getting the place set up. That's what she claimed.

*Or you're trying to figure out where to hide Mama when and if Aunt Vera and Papa do come over,* Darya thought. She'd think things like that even when Aunt Elena was right there in front of her, smiling and practically begging Darya to let her back in. But for the indeterminate future, Darya's heart was shut to Aunt Elena just as it was to Natasha and Mama.

Ava hadn't betrayed her, though. Not yet. She even baked cookies for her. Not tea and jasmine-scented hand cloths, but better!

"I wanted to cheer you up," Ava told her out by the rope swing.

"You did," Darya said with her mouth full. Crumbs spilled out, and she made deliberate lip-smacky sounds. "Nom nom nom! Cookies! From you, because you are the Good Sister!"

Spots of color bloomed on Ava's cheeks. "Don't say that."

"All right. Cookies from you! The Bad Sister!"

"Don't say that either. Darya, come on."

Darya chewed and swallowed. "Yeah, yeah, yeah." She scooted over on the swing's wooden seat and patted the spot beside her. "Come sit with me, Sister of Neutrality. Sister of Switzerland! Come sit, my little Swiss Cake Roll. I am happy with you, and so yes, please, you may join me on my throne."

Ava screwed up her face. "You're weird."

"And you're not? I like that you're weird. I like you, period—as long as you're not here to talk to me about yucky stuff, and I *know* you know what I mean."

Ava squeezed on next to Darya, who pushed against the ground with the toes of her sneakers to get them moving.

"Actually . . ." Ava said timidly.

"No, no. No, no, no," Darya said. "Zip it. Let's just swing."

"But . . . Mama's weird, too. Don't you think? Maybe?"

"Not cool, Ava. Bad transition. Bad segue. Utterly lacking in subtlety, so *boo*. Hush or hop off."

"You said you liked 'weird.' You said it yourself!"

"Did I? No. I said I like *you*, and that you happen

to *be* weird. What is it with people saying I said things I didn't say these days?"

"Huh?" Ava said.

They swung without speaking for several moments. The feeling of moving through the air, forward and back, forward and back, reminded Darya of being a kid.

*You're okay,* she told herself as she and Ava pumped in unison. *Everything's fine. Better than fine, because Ava made cookies!*

Ava cleared her throat. "I just think . . ."

"Do you? Really? Can't we just swing?"

"That we don't know what Mama's gone through," Ava said.

"Fine. We don't. And we don't have to."

"But shouldn't we try?"

Darya stopped pumping. "You know I don't want to talk about this, Ava. Don't make me say something mean."

"I asked Natasha, and it wasn't like you think."

"You don't know what I think," Darya said. She paused. "*What* wasn't like I think?"

"The bad stuff. All of it. Because Mama *didn't* wish for Emily to disappear." Ava sighed. "Will you at least say, 'Okay, I hear you'?"

"Okay, I hear you," Darya said. "But Mama isn't some angel, you know."

"I think she's really lonely and really sad," Ava said. "And it's gross that she smokes, but—"

"Wait. You know that Mama smokes?"

"She's trying to quit. It's hard."

"Have you *seen* Mama? Ava?!"

"Yes, at Aunt Elena's new apartment, which you can come to anytime, you know. Mama misses you. She wants to see you."

"What about Papa? And Aunt Vera?"

"Oh! I think Papa might know! Or almost know, or okay, I don't think he *knows*, but did I tell you about the lady at the art festival?"

Darya didn't like the sound of this. "No."

"She was weird too, but not the good kind. She didn't smoke, but she hung around Papa *all day*."

"And . . . ?"

"Just, why would she, right? She was nice enough, but we didn't *know* her." She paused. "Papa might have known her. He knew her name—*Angela*. But I didn't know her."

"What does this have to do with Mama?"

Ava swung her legs. "What if she's one of Mama's friends? Someone from the olden days? What if Mama sent this Angela to, like, check up on Papa since she's not ready to see him herself?"

Darya blew air out from between her lips, mad at herself for having been baited by Ava's theory for even a moment. "No, Ava, I'm pretty sure Mama isn't using her old friends to spy on Papa. Mama doesn't want anyone to know she's back, remember?"

"But—"

"People at art fairs are friendly. I'm sure she's just Papa's friend, because—was she a vendor or customer?"

"A vendor. She sold bracelets. They were cool, I guess."

"Then see? Papa made a friend, and they probably run into each other at all the art fairs, and I'm glad. I'm *not* glad that Mama still hasn't said, 'Hey look! It's me, your wife!' Why hasn't she?"

Ava made a pouty sound. "It's complicated."

"*Ugh*. I'm so tired of people saying that. How is that an excuse for, like, not doing the right thing?" As she spoke, something beckoned to her from the edge of her thoughts. Then a gust of wind blew the swing forward.

Darya gripped the ropes and turned her head so that she could see her sister's face. Ava kept gazing straight ahead, and Darya watched Ava's eyes change color as the swing swayed through the air. They shifted from brown to tiger's eye golden and back again, with occasional glints of green.

"Did you know that Mama wants me to use my wishes for her?" she said.

Ava showed no reaction, which gave Darya her answer. "Is that such a bad thing?" she asked carefully.

"Ava. They're *my* wishes."

"She doesn't want you to use all of them on her, though. Does she?"

Darya jammed her heels into the ground and brought the swing to a halt. She pushed up from the seat and strode toward the woods. "I'm going for a walk. *Don't* follow me."

Ava hopped off the swing and trotted behind. "Darya, wait. You said you wouldn't be mean."

*Actually, I didn't*, she wanted to say. *I said, "Don't make me be mean."* But what kind of messed-up logic was that?

*Don't* make *me hit you!*

*Don't* make *me make you disappear!*

Her heart pounded. She didn't want to be the sort of person who acted that way *or* thought that way, ever!

She stopped. Briefly, she closed her eyes. When she opened them, she looked at Ava and said, "My bad. I was being a jerk." The next part was harder, but she forced the words out, reminding herself that lying to someone you loved was sometimes kinder than telling the truth—and that truth *wasn't* her jam, anyway.

"If it's that important to you, I'll try to have more of an open mind about Mama," she said.

"You will?" Ava said.

"It's just hard for me, because . . . I don't know. Maybe I'm not as mature as you are about these things?"

"Oh," Ava said uncertainly.

"Yeah. But I love you *so much*, Ava. Just, it would be really great if you could give me some space. Do you think you could do that? Please?"

Ava twisted the bottom of her T-shirt between her fingers. "Um, sure?"

Darya felt a pang. It killed her when Ava was so . . . *Ava*. So sweet and kind and innocent.

"Good," Darya said. "Thanks."

Ava gazed at her for a long moment before heading for the house.

"I do love you!" Darya called.

"Love you, too," Ava echoed, taking odd, careful steps across the yard.

Darya thought maybe Ava would glance over her shoulder to give Darya one last look, but she didn't.

# CHAPTER EIGHTEEN

As Darya's Wishing Day ticked closer, Darya sensed that something inside her needed out. No, was *demanding* to get out. She had so many questions, and so few answers!

If a tree falls in the forest and no one is around to hear it, does it make a sound?

If a mother returns from GONE, is she really back?

If a man once had a sister, and the sister disappeared . . . did the sister ever exist?

*You're making things worse, not better, and it seems an awful lot like you're feeling sorry for yourself,* Darya told herself when these thoughts grew too loud. *So quit it, or else . . . or else . . .*

She couldn't come up with an "or else," so she began to give herself challenges. Or punishments? Distractions, at any rate.

*Don't touch anything brown for the entire day— but don't let anyone notice. If someone notices, you have to start fresh the next day.* No one did notice, which maybe was good, but annoyed Darya nonetheless.

*Don't drink anything, including water from the water fountain, from the time the morning bell rings until after lunch.* That one wasn't as hard as Darya would have liked, although the Coke she swigged once the challenge was over tasted like heaven.

*Don't go to the bathroom for any reason from the time the morning bell rings until after lunch.* That one was dreadful. She should have skipped breakfast, and she certainly should have skipped the tall glass of orange juice. By hour four, she felt sure she was going to burst.

*Go to school with greasy hair, and too bad if people think you've let your standards drop. Don't make excuses. Don't talk about it at all. And no baseball caps or messy buns, either.*

*Hold your breath for a minute. A minute and fifteen*

191

*seconds. A minute and thirty seconds.* Two *minutes.
(You're almost there! Keep going! If you were actually drowning, if you were submerged beneath a sheet
of ice, for example, then you'd have no choice but to
keep going, wouldn't you?)*

She didn't make it to two minutes, though she
lasted long enough that a white light filled her head
and drove all other senses away.

*Not bad*, she told herself, sucking in great gulps of
air. Oxygen rushed through her, a zillion times sweeter
than Coke.

She told herself that these tests, these challenges,
would prepare her for what was coming.

Which was . . . ?

She didn't know.

On rare occasions she sensed the *possibility* of
knowing, as if the answer was there, but hiding, like a
blackbird perched in shadows. But when she brought
her hands together, the blackbird took flight, transformed into a blur of feathers.

On a Monday near the end of October—three
days now from her Wishing Day—she found herself
so burdened by the mysteries of life that she could
hardly function. Or perhaps it was the prior night's

challenge, which was to wake up every hour on the hour and do twenty-five jumping jacks, twenty-five sit-ups, and twenty-five push-ups. Life's mysteries, moonlit calisthenics—both nearly unbearable.

She dragged herself through the school day as best she could, discovering as she did that she *really* didn't do well with sleep deprivation. She stubbed her toe repeatedly. She bumped into walls. She forgot to turn in assignments, and she was so addled that she somehow ended up going to Natasha's English class instead of her own.

She took a seat at the back of the room, puzzled to see Belinda Berry in the desk beside hers. Belinda Berry was fun and popular, the coolest of the cool. Since when was Belinda Berry in Darya's English class?

Then Darya saw Natasha walk into the room with Stanley—and they were holding hands. At school! In front of the universe and Belinda Berry and everyone!

"Natasha!" Darya exclaimed.

Natasha's eyebrows flew up. "Darya? What are you doing here?"

"What am *I* doing here? What are you . . . ?"

She trailed off. Everyone stared at her, Natasha and Stanley included.

"Are you an exchange student?" Belinda asked.

"What?" Darya said. "No!" She got up so abruptly that her knee thwonked the bottom of the desk. A hollow boom reverberated around the room.

"Belinda, that's Darya *Blok*," a girl named Katie said. "Natasha's sister?"

Darya fast-walked out of the room and down the hall. The heels of her boots went *tock-tock-tock*, like a Ping-Pong ball bouncing along the floor.

Later, in her actual English class, Darya wondered what would happen if one day she stopped coming to school altogether. Would Belinda Berry notice, or would she revert to a reality in which Darya Blok had never existed?

Maybe Belinda would decide that Natasha had made Darya up.

Maybe, before Mama learned to keep her mouth shut about her onetime best friend, people thought Mama made Emily up. Who would believe her if she said that actually, and unfortunately, she'd *un*made her?

How was Darya supposed to love someone who did something so horrible?

How could anyone love someone who did something so horrible?

That evening, Darya brought her foul mood home with her and did her best to infest everyone else with it.

At the end of their family dinner, Aunt Vera threw down her napkin in disgust. "Darya, *enough*," she said.

"What?" Darya replied.

"Whatever's troubling you, figure it out," Aunt Vera said. "It's clear you're in one of your moods again, but you need to quit inflicting it on the rest of us."

Papa frowned. "Is something troubling you, Darya?"

"No," Darya protested.

He turned to Natasha. "Natasha? What's going on?" He blinked and gazed around the table. "And where's Elena? Wasn't she . . . didn't she . . . ?"

"She's at her apartment," Natasha said, as if Papa were a child.

"Papa *knows* she doesn't live with us anymore," Darya said angrily. "Just, she promised to keep having Sunday dinners with us. That's what you're talking about, right, Papa?"

"But tonight's not Sunday," Natasha said.

"So?!" Darya demanded.

Papa looked from Natasha to Darya. He drew together his unruly eyebrows, which were threaded with gray. "I . . . I'm confused."

"Of course you are, because everyone in this family is confused," Darya said. "Too bad, so sad."

"Darya!" Aunt Vera snapped. "You are acting disrespectful and rude, and your behavior is unacceptable. Go to your room *now*."

"Fine! Happy to!" Darya shot back, heat rising in her face. She shoved her chair away from the table, hating the fact that the people she loved most didn't have a clue what she was feeling.

Natasha pushed her chair back, too. She followed Darya to the bottom of the staircase and grabbed her shoulder, whipping her around.

"Aunt Vera is already suspicious," Natasha said under her breath. "Do you *want* her to figure things out? About Mama?"

"What if I do? How is keeping her in the dark a better option? How is keeping *Papa* in the dark a better option?"

"Mama needs to tell them herself."

"Then she should tell them! What's stopping her?"

"*You* are, Darya. You know that. You're the only one who can fix things, and she's waiting for you to tell her you will!"

Aunt Vera poked her head into the hall and said,

"Girls! No more bickering! Natasha, back to the table. Darya, *up to your room.*"

⌒

She slept fitfully. The following morning, she woke up with her heart banging. The T-shirt she'd slept in was damp with sweat, and her covers were tangled and half-flung from the bed. She'd dreamed something terrible; she just knew it. Only, she couldn't remember what.

Her bad mood hung over her all day, and when she got home from school, all she wanted was to take a nap. Just as she was about to drift off, Ava knocked on her door.

"What?" Darya snapped.

Ava stepped into her bedroom. Her hairbrush hung from her hand. "You're not mad at *me*, are you?"

"What? No. Why would I be mad at you?"

"I don't know. But I don't know why you're mad at Natasha, either. Or your friends. Are you mad at your friends?"

"Did you want something, Ava? Or are you just here to annoy me?"

"Oh!" She held out her brush. "Will you give me a high ponytail?"

"You want me to do your *hair*? Now? No, do it yourself."

"But you do it so much better," Ava wheedled.

"Because I care about stuff like that. You don't."

"I do so."

"Since when?"

Ava shuffled uncertainly.

"Since *when*, Ava?"

"Never mind. I guess I don't need you to."

In a flash, Darya was up from her bed and had Ava by the wrist. "Ava? What aren't you telling me?"

"Nothing! Stop it! Just, I don't want to be Bumpy Ava!"

"Ex*cuse* me? Who's Bumpy Ava? *What's* a Bumpy Ava?"

"It's fromarmersettanatasha," Ava said, cramming her words together.

"What?"

Ava took a breath. "Mama's letter to Natasha. I didn't mean to bring it up."

"But you did, so you have to explain. She called you 'bumpy'?"

"Not me. Molly."

"Molly as in *Molly*? Natasha's best friend, Molly? Mama left notes for Natasha about *Molly*?"

"Not the notes. I'm talking about the letter, the one she wrote *before* she disappeared."

"Oh, right," Darya said, though this was the first she'd heard of any such letter. She felt wounded and embarrassed and . . . betrayed, but she tried not to show it.

She let go of Ava, took the brush, and started brushing Ava's hair. "Now I understand," she said conversationally. "I don't remember the Molly part, though."

"Well, in kindergarten, people used to call Molly 'Bumpy Molly.'"

"Oh yeah," Darya said, jerking at a tangle. "Why was that, again?"

"*Ouch!* Because Molly's ponytail always had bumps in it. So I don't want to be Bumpy Ava, that's all."

"You won't be, because I don't *do* bumps," Darya said. She gathered Ava's hair in one hand. "Do you have a hair thingie?"

Ava handed her a stretchy loop of ribbon with the word *Gratitude* written across it in swirly letters.

She pulled Ava's hair through the ribbon once, twice, and then half-through again. She left the ends of Ava's hair trapped by the ribbon, creating a poufy loop of hair that dangled halfway down her back.

"Hey," Ava protested, reaching back to touch it.

"It's not bumpy," Darya countered.

Ava freed the ends and shook her hair so that the ponytail hung right, and the exchange made Darya's chest loosen. It was because Darya, whenever she did Ava's hair, *always* left a sneaky ponytail pouf, which Ava *always* immediately depoufed. Darya was comforted by the reminder that some things didn't change.

Ava admired herself in Darya's mirror. "Thanks."

"Yeah, yeah," Darya said. She waved her off.

*Bumpy Molly*, she mused. It was an odd story, because Molly wasn't bumpy now. Molly took a lot of care with her appearance. In fact, hadn't *Molly* called *Natasha* "Bumpy Natasha" at some point?

Yes, she had!

"Let me," Darya recalled Molly insisting when she and Natasha were maybe ten and Darya was nine. Molly had undone Natasha's ponytail and done it over. "You don't want to be Bumpy Natasha."

Natasha had blushed—and remembering it made *Darya* blush.

Why? It wasn't as if Molly had called *Darya* "Bumpy Darya."

Anyway, who cared about being "bumpy"?

Well, lots of people. Girls, at any rate.

But why would Mama include something like that in a letter she wrote eight years ago? And why would Ava know about it, but not Darya?

Darya strode out of her room and down the hall. She barged into Natasha's room.

"Hey!" Natasha protested.

"Did Mama write you a letter before she left?" Darya asked.

"Yeah. So?"

"Did you let Ava read it?"

Natasha looked uncomfortable. "No, but I told her about it. Why?"

"Because you should have told me about it, too. If you told Ava, you have to tell me."

"Actually, I don't," Natasha said. "It's my letter, so I get to decide what to do with it. You can decide what to do with your own letter."

Silence deafened the room.

The color drained from Natasha's face.

"Mama left *two* letters?" Darya said.

Natasha tried to speak. It came out croaky. "Three, actually. One for me, one for you, one for Ava. But we're supposed to read them on the *exact day* of our Wishing Day, and not before. We aren't allowed to read them before."

"How interesting," Darya said, adrenaline surging through her. "But if it's my letter, then I get to decide. Isn't that what you said?" She held out her hand. "Give it to me."

# CHAPTER NINETEEN

"No," Natasha said. "Your Wishing Day isn't till Thursday."

"Two whole days away," Darya said. "Big whup."

"Well, I'm sorry, but I'm going to follow the rules."

"Who made you the big boss? Did you read yours on your exact Wishing Day?" Darya sketched a rough timeline in her head, based on what Natasha had told her. "You couldn't have, because . . . wait, how did you even know about these letters? You didn't start talking to Mama till *after* your Wishing Day."

"Okay, but if I'd known about her letter before-hand, I'd have followed her instructions and read it when she said to."

"Why?"

"What do you mean, why? Because that's what she wanted."

"Would you have changed your wishes? Would you *not* have wished for Mama to come back?"

Visibly, Natasha tried to regroup. "Besides, Mama wanted *Papa* to give them to us. I'm not supposed to be the one."

Natasha's strategic skills needed some work, Darya thought. "Did Papa give you yours?" she asked, adopting a fake-puzzled tone.

"Yes, actually!"

"Really? He just up and gave it to you? Or did you go to him and say, 'Hey, Papa, did Mama by any chance leave a letter for me way long ago? 'Cause if so, I kinda need it, please.'"

Natasha folded her arms over her chest. Her nostrils flared.

From down the hall came the sound of Ava's raised voice. She was addressing a bird—no, *scolding* a bird.

"You need to share with that little bird, you big meanie bird!" Darya heard her little sister say. She was no doubt standing in front of her window, hands on her hips and eyes blazing. It wouldn't be the first time she gave a blue jay—or cat or puppy or squirrel—a piece of her mind. "Sharing is caring!"

Natasha grimaced and rose from her bed. "Let's go outside."

"So we can get my letter?"

"So we can hear each other talk."

Darya grabbed her army jacket and trailed Natasha to the backyard, where yellow and orange leaves covered the ground. The wind stirred among the trees, sending more leaves fluttering down as Aunt Vera came out of the house with a bag of trash. She spotted Natasha and Darya and gave a brisk nod.

"It's about time you two sorted things out," she called.

She opened the metal trash bin and heaved the bag in. When the lid banged shut, several crows cawed and took to flight. The birds in the tree by Ava's bedroom complained as well. Ava raised her voice to compete with them, and Aunt Vera frowned.

"Ava, pipe down!" she scolded. "You're too old to be making such a racket!"

She went back inside, and Darya shook her head. "There's no pleasing that woman. There's always going to be something one of us does that bugs her, isn't there?"

Natasha laughed. Darya shot her a quick sideways glance and allowed herself a cautious smile.

"Hey," she said, because she'd been thinking more about Natasha and Mama, the notes and now the letters. "Those notes Benton Hale left you last year, the ones that turned out not to be from Benton after all. We decided they must have been from Stanley, but they weren't, were they?"

Stanley was the boy Natasha had been holding hands with at school. Stanley was also Benton's best friend. He was adorkable as opposed to adorable, but he was a good guy. After discovering that Natasha's secret admirer wasn't Benton, Stanley—at the time—seemed like the next best fit.

"I thought they were. I even asked him if they were," Natasha admitted. "It was super embarrassing."

"But they were from Mama. Got it. Why won't you let me read them?"

Natasha paced in a tight circle. "Because they're mine. You're worrying about the wrong stuff, Darya. Don't worry about the notes, or the letters; worry about your wishes! You have the power to do something good—"

"*Oh*, the *power*," Darya said, making spooky fingers even as her pulse picked up. She did *not* have the power! She didn't want or accept the power!

"But instead of making things better, you complain. You skulk around and scowl at all of us. You accuse *me* of keeping secrets because I happen to want to keep some things private, but here we are—me and Ava and Mama and Aunt Elena—and we all want to be here for you! But you push us away, and you won't say why, so doesn't that mean you're the one who's hiding something?"

Darya spun on her heel and walked away.

"Where are you going?" Natasha said.

"I'm over it," Darya said. "You and your whole power trip thing. Why do *you* get to call all the shots?"

"I never said I did."

"But that's what you're doing, isn't it?"

An idea struck her. She changed her course.

"Darya?" Natasha called. Darya heard a flurry of footsteps. "Darya!"

"I really am slow, aren't I?" Darya said over her shoulder. "Here I am, begging you for information when all I have to do is go to Papa myself. I'll ask *him* for my letter."

"Darya, don't."

"I mean, sure, he might ask *why*," Darya said. "And it's possible that I might slip up and mention that Mama isn't *gone* after all. She wasn't abducted by aliens, she didn't get amnesia, she wasn't attacked by a serial killer and left to die."

"Nobody ever thought she'd been attacked by a serial killer!" Natasha exclaimed.

"Didn't they?" Darya said, turning and staring at her sister. "*You're* the one who said you thought she might have died, Natasha."

"But not attacked by a serial killer. Anyway, now I know better!"

"I don't know what I know, except that Mama is right here in Willow Hill, in a 'charming garage apartment' with Aunt Elena. Papa doesn't know that, but I could tell him."

"You can be such a brat," Natasha spat.

Darya's stomach cramped. She started for Papa's studio, but Natasha grabbed her.

"No," Natasha commanded. "You win, all right? I'll get you the letter. But you will *not* tell Papa. That's Mama's decision. Not yours."

Darya and Natasha stared at each other. It felt to Darya as if the world was slipping, as if all the pieces could fly apart if she wasn't careful.

Natasha gave Darya a rough shove, then strode to Papa's workshop. She rapped on the door. "Papa, are you in there?"

There was no answer.

Natasha opened the door and went inside. Darya darted across the yard and slipped in behind her. She scanned the workshop to make sure Papa truly wasn't there, and then she breathed in deep, allowing the smell of wood to overwhelm her.

Lutes in various stages of construction filled the room, carved from tangy cedar and sweet-smelling rosewood. According to family lore, Mama used to play the lute. Her fingers would dance over the strings, and she and her sisters, Aunt Vera and Aunt Elena, would sing old Russian folk songs. Papa would sing too, smiling with pride at his beautiful wife.

Papa, happy. It was difficult to imagine.

Natasha went to the back of the workshop, where an antique chest of drawers stood against the wall. She patted the top of the chest.

"What are you doing?" Darya asked.

Natasha whipped her head around. "I told you to wait outside."

"Oops."

Natasha frowned and returned to her task. Her

fingers made purchase on something. A key. She used it to unlock the top drawer of the chest, which she then opened.

"*That's* where the letters are?" Darya said.

"Not mine. Just yours and Ava's."

"Wow. Great hiding spot."

Natasha pulled a sealed envelope from the drawer. It was made of creamy card stock. Across the front was Darya's name in graceful, elegant cursive.

Natasha closed the drawer, locked it, and put back the key. She crossed the floor and offered Darya the letter. When Darya didn't take it, Natasha shrugged and moved as if to return the letter.

Darya snatched it. "Thanks so very much for giving me what was mine already!" she called as she hurried out of Papa's workshop. Her eyes filled with tears— why? *why?!*—and she strode half-blindly across the backyard, into the woods, and to the path that led to town.

*Get away*, her footfalls said. *Away, away, away.*

In her head spoke another voice, the voice of a little girl: *If I tell you a riddle, will you stay?*

She shook the voice out, but it found the rhythm of her feet as they slapped the trail. *Stay and stay and stay! Go away, away, away!*

She was going crazy! It was really and truly happening! Birds crowded her skull, their stubby wings pumping. She wanted to scream. She couldn't scream. *She must not scream.* She was going to scream whether she wanted to or not!

Then—peace, or a measure of it, gradually came to her as she stopped still, held her breath, and counted.

*One, two, three . . .*

The noise between her ears died down. The need to scream receded.

*Thirty-four, thirty-five, thirty-six. Thirty-seven, thirty-eight, thirty-nine. You can do this, Darya. You can.*

The birds flew from her skull.

*Seventy-two, seventy-three.*

She was liquefying from the inside. She would burst if she didn't get air.

*Make it to seventy-five. You've done that before.*

She made it to a hundred.

*Now a hundred. Come on. Don't give up!*

She clenched her letter. She closed her eyes.

*A hundred and one, a hundred and two . . .*

It was her farthest yet! And she'd been right, her tests *had* been preparing her for something, and surely this was it!

At a hundred and four—one minute and forty-four seconds!—the white light flooded her senses and drove everything else away. Her eyelids fluttered. She nearly dropped Mama's letter.

Then, in a wonderful *whoosh*, she let her stale breath out. She sucked fresh air in, clean and crisp and scented with the same tang she'd smelled in Papa's workshop.

Her mind was clear. She could think again, and thank goodness, because she needed to think.

She also needed to open Mama's letter, and she would! Obviously!

So why resist it? Why didn't she rip it open right this second?

*Because what if it doesn't say what you want it to say?* a small voice whispered. *What if it doesn't fix things?*

She grimaced, remembering the other small voice. The little girl's voice. *If I tell you a riddle, will you—*

NO. Not helpful.

She started walking, tapping the envelope that held Mama's letter against her open palm. The envelope was sealed, and that was a plus. The pages wouldn't spill out of their own accord.

As she walked, she ran things over in her mind,

and she realized that she needed a plan. Obviously! And the reason she needed a plan was this: before she did anything, she had to sort herself out. *Then* she would open Mama's letter. She'd be stronger. She'd be prepared. She'd be able to handle whatever the letter said, whether good, bad, or neutral.

What needed sorting out was . . . well, she had no easy answer for that. So many things needed sorting out. What she mulled over now was her encounter with the Bird Lady, way back on the afternoon of her birthday. The memory was tender, so she prodded it gingerly, like exploring a sore spot in her mouth with the tip of her tongue.

*Feeling sorry for yourself will hardly help*, the Bird Lady had told Darya, after ambushing her on the way home from the library. *If you don't like your life, maybe you should change it.*

Darya had argued that she liked her life just fine, which had made the Bird Lady practically roll her eyes. And then had come the weird part, which had been *so* weird that Darya had decided to block it from her thoughts altogether.

*But things leak out.*

Wasn't that what the Bird Lady had said?

It was. Of course it was. If Darya lied about it now,

she'd be lying to herself, and maybe she was growing tired of such childish behavior.

She kept walking, steadying her breaths and regulating her gait.

*Think about something else*, she told herself. *Just for a moment, to give your mind a break.*

She felt the wind on her body and shivered, glad she'd thought to throw on her army jacket. Her army jacket! She loved her army jacket.

*Think about that, then*, she told herself.

Its cut was narrow and flattered her slender figure. Delicate vines meandered up the sleeves, embroidered in olive thread that was one shade darker than the fabric. The vines were so subtle that most people didn't notice them. Darya, in her thirteen years, had concluded that most people failed to notice most things.

But Darya loved the vines. She also loved how broken-in her jacket was, how its sleeves were frayed and how loose stitches straggled from their edges. It made her feel both pretty and tough.

Tough enough, in fact, to let her thoughts drift back to her run-in with the Bird Lady.

She prodded that strange memory again, and this time it opened itself up to her like a tulip whispering secrets into the bud of her ear.

Fireflies in a jar, their bodies butting against the glass.

A lid twisted tight.

Spells, as in magic. *Magic* magic, at least as seen through the Bird Lady's ancient eyes. Spells and magic and . . . expiration dates?

It came to Darya then, and once it did, there was no shaking it free.

*You were six, and you wore a dress with cherries on it, and you asked me for a Forgetting Spell*, the Bird Lady had said, studying Darya keenly. *Do you remember now?*

She'd said she hadn't, but she kind of did. Almost.

It had to do with Mama. She was sure of that.

Perhaps it had to do with Mama's letter?

Darya's skin felt clammy. Her pace had grown slower and slower without her noticing, until she was practically slithering along. A snail. A girl-shaped snail, clammy and full of ooze.

*Ick.*

She shuddered and walked faster, flipping up her army jacket and tucking Mama's letter into the back pocket of her jeans. She would find Tally, whose life was as tangled in darkness as her own. Maybe Tally didn't know her as well as Natasha or Ava or Aunt

Elena, all of whom were so eager, according to Natasha, to "be there" for her. But shouldn't Darya have a say in who was there for her, and when?

Anyway, Darya and Tally were members of the Missing Daughters Club. Tally would listen sympathetically. Best of all, Tally wouldn't add any new twists to the story—secret letters, undercover rendezvous, whatever—because Tally wasn't part of the story.

So, Darya would talk to Tally. She'd share what she wanted to share—no more, no less—and she'd get herself sorted out.

*Then* she'd open Mama's letter.

# CHAPTER TWENTY

To find out where Tally lived, Darya went to the library, strode to the reference desk, and pulled out Willow Hill's ridiculously thin phone book. She felt old-school cool looking the address up by hand instead of using a computer. She rifled through the pages until she found an entry for *Kaufman, Deanne. 45 Magnolia Lane*, she read. Easy-peasy lemon squeezy.

Nosy Ms. McKinley swished over in her overstuffed nylons and matronly dress, and Darya flipped the phone book shut.

"Can I help you?" Ms. McKinley asked, smelling strongly of bottled flowers.

"No thanks," Darya said.

"Who were you looking up?"

"No one," Darya said.

Ms. McKinley pursed her lips. Then she switched gears and smiled. Her lips were bright red, and there was a piece of food caught between two of her back teeth. A piece of flesh, from the looks of it.

"Well, what news do we have of your mother?" she asked.

"'We'?" Darya said. She screwed up her face to say, *I don't get it. What do you mean, "we"?*

Ms. McKinley huffed. The piece of meat swayed, and Darya had a difficult time dragging her eyes off it. "Have we—have *you*—heard from your mother at all?"

Darya made an elaborate show of grasping the librarian's intent, widening her eyes and saying, "*Ohhhhh.* My mom. You're wondering if she's been in touch? Actually . . ."

Darya leaned close. Ms. McKinley leaned closer.

"Can you keep it a secret? What I'm about to tell you?" Darya whispered.

With wide mascaraed eyes, Ms. McKinley nodded. She looked like she might wet herself, she was that excited. "Absolutely!" she whispered back.

"Well . . ." Darya started. She bit her bottom lip and gave herself anxious eyes.

"Oh honey, you can tell me anything," Ms. McKinley urged.

"*Anything?*"

"*Anything!*" Ms. McKinley said, and she actually circled her hand to say, *Go on, then. Spill!*

"In that case, there is one thing I can tell you, and I *guess* you can share it if you feel like it's, you know, safe." She dropped her Anxious Girl Act. "When I want to share information about my mother with you—which, for the record, will be never—I'll tell you straight to your face. Which looks remarkably like a pudding. Got it?"

Ms. McKinley gasped and put her hand to her heart. Her pudding-face turned a mottled red, and her mascaraed eyes went beady, like tiny round spiders with enormous legs.

"This!" she spluttered. She jabbed her finger at Darya. "This! *You!* Your manners are abominable!"

"'Abominable.' Nice word."

"Although we all know why, don't we? Given that you were raised without a mother!"

"If you say so," Darya replied. "What's your excuse?"

Ms. McKinley choked on her own spit, and Darya strolled past her and out of the library.

When she arrived at 45 Magnolia Lane, she saw a small house with a smaller yard. Junk overflowed from both.

In the yard, Darya spotted four yellow-and-red Big Wheels, two pull-along wagons, and a liberal scattering of naked Barbie dolls, Matchbox cars, and an assortment of other toys. Also a blue plastic pool with green slime growing along the inner edge. Also a plastic play structure that might have been fun if Tally had been two, and if she didn't mind the absence of the slide. Two hinges jutted out where a slide used to be, but from the amount of dirt accumulated on them, Darya suspected the slide itself had been gone for years.

In the house, rising higher than the windows, Darya saw teetering stacks of boxes, newspapers, and magazines. There was other stuff, too, but Darya would have had to cup her hands around her face and peer through the grimy panes to make out what it was.

She lifted her hand to knock on the door, but Tally inched it open before Darya's knuckles hit the wood, or fake wood, or whatever the door was made of.

"Darya, what are you doing here?" she asked, her eyes huge within her pale face. She slid through the crack and shut the door behind her.

"I came to see you," Darya said. "To talk to you."

"You couldn't talk to me at school?"

"What happened didn't happen till after school. Can you talk or not?"

Tally made a *tch* sound. "Fine, but not here." She fast-walked away from the house.

Darya trotted to catch up. "Where are we going? Don't you need to tell your foster mom?"

"Starbucks. We can go there. And no, I don't need to tell anyone, but thanks for asking."

Darya felt stung by Tally's tone. They walked without speaking until they reached the coffeehouse.

"Sorry," Tally said gruffly. "Deanne's house is kind of . . . messy, that's all."

"It's not so bad," Darya said.

Tally arched her brows, then pushed through the Starbucks door. Starbucks was a new addition to Willow Hill, and Darya had been inside only once. The shiny interior intimidated her, as did the friendly— so friendly!—baristas. As did the fact that *they were baristas*!

At the Bluebird Diner, there were just waitresses, and they served coffee, not fancy drinks Darya didn't know how to decode. At the Bluebird Diner, Darya could get pancakes jubilee, not a Slow-Roasted Ham, Swiss, and Egg Breakfast Sandwich or Bacon-Wrapped Dates or a Gluten-Free Marshmallow Dream Bar.

Although all of those sounded good, except for the Gluten-Free Marshmallow Dream Bar.

Tally, on the other hand, seemed at ease inside Starbucks. Her shoulders relaxed. She no longer buzzed with angry energy.

"Want something?" she asked Darya, breezing up to the counter.

"Um, I don't have any money."

Tally pulled out her wallet and withdrew a shiny gold Starbucks card, which she wiggled. "My treat."

Darya scanned the menu again. "Um . . . something without a hyphen?"

Tally looked at Darya, then at the menu, which was above them behind the counter. Then she laughed. "They'll make it however you want. You can order it hyphen-free."

"Okay, then the Old-Fashioned Glazed Doughnut, hyphen on the side. Please."

Tally ordered it just like that. For herself, she ordered something called an Undertow. It involved espresso and cream, and Tally threw back her head and downed it in one quick shot.

"Impressive," Darya commented.

"I try," Tally said.

They sat at a high table far from the door. Darya's legs dangled from the tall stool. It made her feel like a little kid.

"So what's up?"

Darya's thoughts flew to Mama's letter, which hopefully wasn't getting crumpled in her back pocket. But it would be rude, wouldn't it, to dive right in with *me, me, me*?

"How's your day been?" she asked.

Tally looked at her funny. "How's my day been since we saw each other two hours ago? Fine."

"Do anything cool?"

"There's a sketch I'm working on. Water droplets on a blade of grass. I've been trying to figure out how to capture the way light behaves within something transparent."

"Yeah?" Darya said. She tried to come up with something to contribute. "Um . . . pastels or pencil?"

"Graphite. Darya, you couldn't care less about how to draw water droplets."

"I do! I really do!"

Darya wasn't sure, but she thought she saw a change in Tally's eyes. She continued to hold Darya's gaze, but something turned off inside them, sort of.

"All right, maybe I don't," Darya admitted. "But I *do* care about your art. I wish I were as talented as you. I feel like it would . . . give my life purpose, kind of."

"Is that why we're here, to discuss your life's purpose?"

"No, because I don't have a life's purpose. Yet."

"Then . . . ?"

Darya fidgeted on her stool. She let some time slide between them.

"It's been a strange afternoon," she said. "And a strange week before that, and a strange couple of months before that."

"So, ever since your birthday?"

"I guess."

"All right," Tally said. "Strange how?"

"Ms. McKinley called me an abomination. She's the librarian. Not at school, at the public library."

"An abomination?"

"And . . . before I tell you, you have to promise not to say a word to anyone. Not anyone, I mean it."

Their eyes met and caught, and the promise was given and received and understood. They were different, the two of them. They were alike in their difference, and it bound them together.

"My mom's back," Darya said. "She came back. My mom. She's here, in Willow Hill."

"She's here? In Willow Hill? Darya, that's awesome!"

"Is it?"

"When did you find out? Have you seen her? Where was she during all that time she was gone?"

"I have, and it was . . . it wasn't what I thought it would be like. And I don't know where she was. She didn't say."

Tally studied her. "By 'it wasn't what you thought,' do you mean bad?"

"Not bad, but . . ." The words formed in her brain, and she had just enough time to acknowledge her own hypocrisy before hearing herself say, "It's complicated."

"Most families are," Tally said. "Tell me."

Darya broke off a bite of her doughnut, which she crumbled into pieces, littering the clean Starbucks table. She broke off another bite and haltingly told Tally about finding out from Natasha that Mama was back in town and most of what had happened since.

She left out the bits about the Bird Lady and the Forgetting Spell, as those details were prickly and just for herself. She made a point of including the bad stuff, however: Mama's new smoking habit; her abrupt, jittery movements; the depressing, trash-filled swimming pool at the motel she'd stayed at, which was far grosser than Tally's foster mom's house. Only after painting this grim picture did she tell Tally the worst part of all: that Mama wanted Darya to use her Wishing Day wishes to fix Mama's past mistakes.

"But that's ridiculous, right?" Darya said. "And selfish! Parents are supposed to be the grown-ups. *They're* supposed to take care of *us*, the kids."

"Ha, ha," Tally said. "Good one."

Darya checked Tally's expression. "She wore red lipstick the day I saw her, so *maybe* she was making an effort. And she doesn't live in the crappy motel anymore. But why are you looking at me like that? You are on my side, right?"

"What's your side?"

"That I shouldn't use my wishes on her! That they're *my* wishes, so I should use them on *me*. Right?"

"So now you *are* going to do the whole ritual-tradition-thing? Couldn't you do both?"

"No! Maybe! I don't know. Just say, 'You're right, Darya. Of course you are.'"

"You're right, Darya. Of course you are."

Darya scowled. She reached behind her, threaded

her hand past her coat to her back pocket, and pulled out Mama's letter, which she slapped on the table. Doughnut crumbs bounced and skittered.

"She left this."

Tally looked at it. Then she looked at Darya.

"It's a letter. She wrote it *before* she left. Meaning, she knew she was going to leave, but she still took time to write me a letter. She wrote one to each of my sisters, too."

"And that's a bad thing?"

"Yes! Kind of! Because—" She broke off, frustrated that she didn't understand the workings of her own heart.

Tally waited.

"I think it was me," Darya confessed at last, voicing her most shameful fear.

"I don't understand."

"I think I did something. I'm not sure what. But . . . I'm the reason my mom left. Please don't tell anyone!"

"I would never," Tally said. "But Darya, you know that can't be true."

"And I think . . . I think that's why my mom's fine with using my wishes. It's the only way I can make sense of it. She thinks I owe her—and maybe I do!"

"Darya, stop. You're flipping out."

"Am I? How do you know?"

"You can't remember what you did, but whatever it was, *that's* what drove your mom away? You told me you were five when she left, Darya. You were five, and your mom was a grown woman, and yet *you* drove her away?"

"How do you know I didn't?"

"Because I *do*," Tally said. "Omigod, you're acting like every single kid in the world who blames herself for her parents' divorce or whatever. 'Did I not put my toys away? Did I whine too much? Was I so awful that I ruined everything?'"

Darya swallowed. Was Tally still thinking about Darya, or had she gone to her own dark place? Surely Tally didn't blame herself for own mom's messed-up life . . . did she?

Darya tapped the envelope with Mama's letter on it against the table. "The thing is . . . what if it's right here? The truth. About everything."

"You haven't read it?"

Darya shook her head.

"Your *mom* left you a letter, and you haven't *read* it?"

"I'm scared."

228

Tally's eyes flashed. "Too frickin' bad! Oh my God, I can't even . . ." She slashed the air with her hand. "Oh my *God*, Darya!"

"You're not helping," Darya whispered. "Just . . . what should I do?"

"As opposed to moping around doing nothing? Here's a thought—*read your mom's letter.*" She flung herself back in her chair. "My mom hasn't written or called or texted in over a year. I tried to visit her in the treatment facility before I got sent here—that's what they call it, a *treatment facility*—and she told the nurses 'No visitors.' To *me*. And here your mom is, reaching out, and maybe she's not perfect, but who is?!"

Darya stood up. She grabbed Mama's letter and shoved it back in her pocket, and announced shakily that she was going to the bathroom.

In the ladies' room, she splashed cold water on her face. Then she dried her skin with a rough paper towel. She peed, holding Mama's letter in place when she tugged her jeans down and securing the letter again when she finished. She washed her hands. She dragged everything out, half hoping the table would be vacant when she returned. But Tally was still there.

Darya's pulse jumped all over the place as she took a seat on her stool. Not sure if it would make things better or worse, but unable to think of a better idea, she said, "Well . . . so tell me about her. Your mom. Tell me a *happy* memory about her."

Tally narrowed her eyes.

"Maybe I *am* selfish. Maybe I *am* a coward. I'm sure I am!" Darya said. "But . . . we're in this together. Kind of. The Missing Daughters Club, remember? So come on, one happy memory."

Tally thought for several long moments. "I can't think of anything. Sorry."

"Yes, you can. What about decorating the house for Christmas or making cookies together or something?"

The fire in Tally's eyes dimmed, replaced with resignation. "Sure. Yeah. We did decorate Christmas cookies once."

"And was it fun?"

"It was great."

"Well . . . see?"

There was a beat.

"I'm not trying to make everything be about me," Darya said.

"I know. And I'm not trying to always say that I've got it worse."

"But you probably do," Darya admitted.

"Who knows?" Tally said wearily. "It's not a contest either of us should want to win."

Outside the coffeehouse, before they parted ways, Tally lightly traced the embroidered vine on Darya's jacket. "Has that always been there?"

"The vine? Yeah."

"You wear that jacket all the time. How have I never noticed?"

Darya shrugged.

"It's really pretty," Tally said.

"Thanks," Darya said. "And thanks for talking to me, or listening, or whatever. For telling me to read my mom's letter. I will, all right?"

Tally squinted.

"As soon as I get home. I swear!"

"Did the librarian really call you an abomination?"

"Huh? Well, she called me *abominable*. Same difference."

"Why?"

"I don't know. 'Cause I am?"

"No. Or if *you* are, then *I* am, only a thousand times worse."

"No, you're not. Why would you say that?"

Tally gnawed on her lower lip.

"Tally, what?"

Tally looked worried, which made Darya worried. Then smoothed her features and said, "Nothing."

"Tally . . ."

"No, seriously, I have no idea what I was going to say."

They embraced awkwardly and went their own ways. As Darya walked, she thought about bravery and fear, pain and regret. She thought about all that was known and all that wasn't. She thought about mothers. Fathers, too, and aunts and sisters. But mainly mothers.

Halfway there, she reached back to pat the bulge of Mama's letter, which she *would* read as soon as she was in the privacy of her room. She'd said she would, and she would.

Except . . . what the crap?

She patted again. She patted the other pocket. She pushed her jacket aside and twisted around, contorting her body to see for herself.

She felt very hot, then very cold. The letter was gone.

*I wish I could take it back.*

—TALLY STRIKER, AGE THIRTEEN AND A HALF

# CHAPTER TWENTY-ONE

She raced back to Starbucks, scanning the ground with wide desperate sweeps. No letter. She went inside the Starbucks and searched on and around the high table she and Tally had sat at. She searched the ladies' room, too. No letter.

She asked the people sitting nearby if they'd seen it. She asked the barista, too.

"I lost a really important letter," she said desperately. "Maybe someone turned it in?"

"I'm so sorry, but no," the barista said.

Darya was afraid she was going to cry. She stumbled back outside and thought—*the Bird Lady!* It made no sense, but once the idea had landed, Darya couldn't shake it off.

Two months ago, on Darya's birthday, the Bird Lady had warned of memories leaking out. Did a letter count as a memory, if the letter was old and practically forgotten?

*And* she'd asked if Darya remembered the Forgetting Spell that Darya had supposedly requested. Back then, she'd answered no. Because, please.

But now, as she walked distractedly back home, Darya couldn't stop pairing the two things together: Mama's letter and this Forgetting Spell, which, if Darya was honest with herself, didn't seem quite as impossible as she'd tried to tell herself.

*"Impossible,"* the Bird Lady had said on Darya's birthday. "You're fond of that word, aren't you?"

What if Darya *had* asked for a Forgetting Spell?

It sounded ridiculous. It *was* ridiculous!

And yet, she couldn't find her mother's letter.

She went over it and over it. Natasha had given her the letter in Papa's workshop. Rich, creamy card stock, the envelope thick and padded. *Darya* penned across the front. Darya had put it in the back pocket of her jeans, because she had places to go and people

236

to see. Information to hide from, despite repeatedly insisting that she just wanted answers.

She should have read the letter the minute she had it in her hot little hands. But she hadn't, and now it was gone. She hadn't acted; she'd just talked and talked and talked, *blah blah blah*, like Tally said.

She was *so* stupid. God, she was stupid!

She saw a jogger ahead of her, a young woman with her hair pulled back and earbuds in her ears.

"Excuse me!" Darya said. She stepped into the woman's path and waved her hand.

The woman looked startled. She pulled one earbud out and said, while jogging in place, "Do you need help? Are you lost?"

"*I'm* not, but . . . have you seen a letter, by any chance?"

"A *letter?*"

"Yeah. On the trail, maybe?"

"Sorry, no," the woman said, and jogged off.

"Don't you want to ask me?" an old woman asked.

Darya yelped, then clapped her hand over her mouth. She glanced all around to make sure no one else was going to pop out of nowhere before saying, "Omigosh, you *scared* me!"

"Did I, pet?" the Bird Lady inquired.

"Yes, you did, and you meant to!" Darya said, knowing it was true. "Where did you even come from?"

The Bird Lady tapped her chin. "Ah, an excellent question. If we start at the beginning, I suppose you might say that I came from—"

"Never mind!" Darya said quickly. The Bird Lady was *here*, in front of her, the one person in the world who might know the truth about certain secrets from Darya's past. Sure, Darya was interested in the answer to life, the universe, and everything. But that could wait.

"Hmmph," the Bird Lady said. "The short version is that you summoned me."

"I did? I'm pretty sure I didn't."

"I can't always come, but I will when I can."

"What?" Darya said. "No. Forget all that. Could we just talk like normal people, please?"

The Bird Lady cocked her head. "I don't know. How do you define normal?"

Darya wanted to cry out in frustration. She wanted to grab the Bird Lady and shake her.

Instead, she reminded herself of the challenges she'd taken on: don't touch anything brown, don't drink any water, hold your breath and don't let go. Those challenges had taught her self-discipline, hadn't they? Maybe this was what she'd been preparing for.

Evening was coming on, and the light was dimming into purples and blues. Darya moved to the side of the path in case anyone else came along. The Bird Lady lifted her eyebrows and joined her.

"All right, shoot," she said.

Darya took a deep breath. "My mother's letter. Do you have it?"

The Bird Lady drew herself up. "Of course not. You, of all people, should know better than that."

*Should I?* thought Darya. She no longer had any clue about what she "should" or "shouldn't" know.

"Okay, well, did you know my mother's back in town?"

"Obviously."

"Did you know she didn't come home? That she's back in Willow Hill, but that she's not staying at our house. *Her* house. Did you know that?"

"Obviously."

Darya counted to ten. She folded her arms over her chest. "She wants me to use her wishes for her. One of them, anyway."

239

"And?"

And Mama had taken so much from Darya already! How could she give anything more away? "I don't want to," she said.

"And?"

Darya made an impatient sound, which she cut off midway through. "Aren't you going to tell me I should? That it's my duty?"

"Is it?"

"How should I know?"

"Calm down, chicken," the Bird Lady said, which aggravated Darya immensely because she *was* calm. She was so calm she was about to explode!

"If we have the ability to help others, then I believe we should, yes," the Bird Lady said.

"But—"

"Hold on, now. I also believe there's a great deal to be said for doing all we can for ourselves, instead of relying on others to do things for us."

"Okay, so you're saying that—"

"I *also* believe that sometimes, parents can do for their children what they can't do for themselves." The Bird Lady eyed her sternly.

"Please tell me what that means!" Darya said.

The Bird Lady made the motion of checking her

watch. Except she wasn't wearing a watch. "You may ask me one last question."

"Why only one?"

"Is that your question?"

"No. No!" Darya thought hard. She wanted to ask about Emily, but she couldn't figure out how to formulate a single question that could tackle all she needed to know. She wanted to ask where Mama's letter was, but what if the Bird Lady didn't know?

At last she decided to ask the one question that the Bird Lady and only the Bird Lady could answer. She phrased it well before speaking. She checked for loopholes.

"On my birthday, you told me that when I was six, I asked you for a Forgetting Spell," she said. "That's not my question. That's a statement."

"La, la, you know grammar. Look at you!"

"Back when I was six, when I asked you for the spell, what did I want to forget?"

The Bird Lady smiled as if she were pleased. "Think outside the box, pet," she said. "And now, I'm off. Cheerio! Best of luck! Don't give up the fight!"

"I'm not . . . what fight?" Darya called to her retreating figure. "And how is what you just said an answer?!"

"It's not. It's a hint!" the Bird Lady called back, and she disappeared around a bend in the path. *Poof!* It was almost like magic, if the deepening gloom of dusk could be considered magic.

# CHAPTER TWENTY-TWO

Natasha pulled Darya into the laundry room as soon as she returned from town. "So?" she said. "What did it say?"

"What did what say?" Darya replied, trying to buy time.

"You know what I'm talking about," Natasha said. "The letter from Mama!"

"*Ohhhhh.* That. Um . . . lots of things. So many. But, to quote someone who thinks she's very wise, it's my letter, so I get to decide what to do with it. And I'm going to keep it private."

Natasha looked puzzled, and then hurt. But what

else could Darya do? Admit she'd lost it?

After dinner, Darya slipped outside and sat on the swing, gripping the rope handles and tilting her face to the waxing moon. In two days—or two nights—the moon would be full. Papa had a *Farmer's Almanac*, which was a book that listed such things. During the day of October thirtieth, the temperature would most likely be in the sixties; during the night, it would dip into the forties. There'd be a thirty percent chance of gusting winds.

Also on October thirtieth, Darya would have to decide whether or not to honor the Wishing Day tradition. Although she wouldn't necessarily have to let anyone else in on her decision, she supposed.

*If a tree falls in the forest, but no one is around to hear it, does it make a sound?*

*If a girl makes three wishes, but no one serves as a witness, will the wishes come true?*

*If a girl comes back from GONE, a girl named Emily, for example . . . is she truly back?*

A screech owl hooted, and Darya scurried back inside, reminding herself to relax her shoulders and hold her chin high. *I'm cool, everything's cool. Nothing to see here, people.*

244

She dreamed that night of an enormous owl that swooped down and caught her in its talons. The owl spirited her away—good-bye, sisters, good-bye, home, good-bye, Papa, all alone—and an endless sky swallowed her up.

~

The next day was a teacher workday, so there was no school. Darya called Tally and said, "I need to talk to you."

"I know," Tally said.

"You do? Oh. Well, can we meet? Back at Starbucks in, say, half an hour?"

"I can get there quicker."

"Then, sure. See you soon."

She fast-walked to town, but Tally was already standing outside the coffeehouse when she arrived. She waved Darya over, and Darya flashed on the Bird Lady's hint.

*Think outside the box*, the Bird Lady had said.

*How about outside of the Starbucks?* Darya wondered. *Outside the Bux?*

"No, no, and no," she muttered to herself. She waved at Tally and rushed over. When they were within two feet of each other, they both started talking.

245

"Omigosh, thank you so much for coming," Darya said, while at the same time, Tally said, "Darya, I am *so* sorry."

They blinked at each other.

"Of course," Tally said.

"For what?" Darya said.

Tally had circles under her eyes, and her blotchy skin suggested she'd been rubbing at it. Maybe crying?

"Tally, what's wrong?"

Tally pulled a rumpled envelope from the backpack slung over her shoulder. Darya peered at it, then gasped and flung her arms around Tally.

"You found it!" she cried. "You are the best friend ever!" She let go of Tally and took the letter. *Mama's* letter, still sealed, with "Darya" written in Mama's own handwriting across the front. Darya bounced on her toes. "Omigosh, where *was* it?"

Tally didn't answer, and Darya's smile fell away as she put the pieces together. Blotchy skin. Tired eyes. *Darya, I'm so sorry.*

"You . . . took it?" Darya said.

Tally nodded miserably.

Darya's stomach dropped so hard and so fast that she thought she might throw up. She checked again to make sure it was sealed. Truly sealed, not opened sneakily with a knife and glued shut again.

"I didn't touch it!" Tally said.

"Well, you *did*. Um, you stole it from me, so guess what? That counts as touching it."

Tally flushed a dark, painful red. "You're right. I'm sorry. I didn't *read* it, I promise."

"And your promise means . . . ? Wow, not too much, does it?" She heard how dispassionate she sounded and marveled at herself. Then an aching lump rose in her throat, and she couldn't fake it anymore. Whimpering puppy noises wrenched themselves from her chest.

"Darya . . ."

Darya cried harder. She thought of her tests, her challenges, and how she'd succeeded at all of them, and still her friend had stolen from her. No test could have prepared her for this.

"Why?" she managed, her voice thick.

"I don't know."

"You do so."

Tally's eyes darted from side to side. "Can we go inside? I'll buy you a coffee."

"No."

"Or a doughnut! Do you want a doughnut?"

"No."

She gestured to the curb in front of the coffeehouse. "Can we at least sit down?"

"*No*. We can stand right here, and you can tell me why you thought it was all right to stick a knife into my heart and twist it. Because that's what it feels like, Tally."

Tally didn't answer.

Darya turned on her heel and started furiously across the parking lot.

"Darya! Wait!"

She heard the slap of Tally's tennis shoes.

"You have *so* much," Tally said. "You have no idea how lucky you are."

"So you've told me, and sure. Absolutely. I'm so *lucky* to have a backstabbing friend who steals from me." Her breath hitched. "Did you want to punish me? Is that it?"

"Yes, actually!" Tally said. She started crying, too. "But that was so so wrong of me."

"You think?"

"You seemed to be wasting it, that's all."

"Wasting what? The letter you stole?"

"No. Yes. Everything!" She reached for Darya. Darya shrugged her off. "Darya, you don't want to hear this, and it doesn't make what I did right, but your mom might not be the bad guy you want her to be."

"I want my mom to be the 'bad guy'? That's just . . . that's messed up."

"She smokes! Oh no! There are bigger problems a mom can have than being a smoker."

Darya fished for a retort, but found herself imagining Tally at . . . at the treatment facility or wherever, trying to visit her mom and being turned away.

She strode off, clutching Mama's letter. She had it back, and that was what mattered. She'd be reading it in ten minutes or less.

"The thing is, I think you're afraid," Tally said, hop-skipping to match Darya's pace.

"Oh yeah? The thing *is*, you don't get to tell me what you think." She swallowed. "Well, you can. I just don't have to listen."

"And maybe you feel, like, inadequate?"

Darya shot Tally a look of disbelief. "*You're* inadequate. Stealing things is very inadequate. And who says 'inadequate,' anyway?"

"My therapist," Tally said.

"You have a therapist?"

"I've had lots of therapists."

Darya was a wreck, but she wasn't heartless. But also she wondered if it was fair, Tally throwing out *I've had lots of therapists* so matter-of-factly.

Well, not matter-of-factly. Tally was as teary as Darya was. Whatever.

"I'm sorry that *you* are afraid and that *you* feel inadequate," Darya said. She sniffled. "And no doubt I should be the one going to a therapist, and maybe one day I will. But today? Please just leave."

"Darya . . ."

From the side of her eye, Darya saw Tally stop walking. Darya clenched her jaw and kept going. She continued on for several steps before whirling around.

Tally held out her hands. "I gave it back, didn't I?"

Darya clenched her jaw. Tally won no awards for giving back something she stole.

"As for your mom . . ." Tally's voice cracked. "What if she leaves again? And what if this time it *is* your fault, because you could have stopped her and you didn't even try?"

"I *did* try to stop her!" Darya bellowed. "She left anyway!"

Tally's mouth fell open. Darya swayed, light-headed from a swirl of confusion. Where had those words come from? What long-buried memory had risen and bubbled out, only to evaporate the instant it reached open air?

The world went blurry, and Darya ran. She had to get away from Tally. She had to get home. She ran faster and faster until her heart banged against her ribs and her breath rasped within her lungs. She ran until she reached the backyard. She ran past Papa's workshop, past the rope swing, and—*smack*. Right into Natasha.

# CHAPTER TWENTY-THREE

"Darya!" Natasha said. "Are you okay?"

Darya reeled back and stumbled, falling on her tailbone. "Ow! Sheesh! What are you doing?"

"Looking for you! We had that . . . fight last night . . . and I wanted to make up."

*Oh, Natasha, not now,* she thought hopelessly. "Well . . . thanks. But we're good. Really."

"You don't look good. You look teary." Natasha peered at her. "Oh, wow. *Are* you teary?"

"No. I'm sweaty, but I'm not teary. I . . . went for a run."

"A run?"

"Uh-huh, to be healthy."

Natasha extended a hand, and Darya reluctantly took it. Natasha pulled her to her feet.

"Is that Mama's letter?" Natasha said, her focus narrowing on Darya's free hand.

"Actually . . . yes."

Natasha twisted Darya's forearm to get a better view, and her eyes widened. "You haven't opened it? But . . . you said . . ."

"I didn't say anything, really. Not anything that mattered. But I don't want to fight with you anymore, so could we just . . . not?"

Natasha let go of Darya. "But Darya . . ."

*I am* afraid, *Darya thought. I am* inadequate.

"There's something Mama wanted to tell you, but you never let her," Natasha said. "And tomorrow's your Wishing Day."

"Yep, it sure is."

"So I decided that I should tell you. Will you let me?"

"Not today. Not now. I *really* can't take it right now."

"It's just, Emily was more than Papa's little sister. Emily was—"

"Natasha, please," Darya said. Her vision blurred,

and her anger seeped away as all of her failings rose up inside her. "Listen, I'll use my wishes well. I'll do something good."

Natasha's eyes widened. "You will?"

Darya spread her arms. *Yes,* she hoped that her gesture implied. *Here I am telling you yes, so will you please stop telling me stuff?*

"Darya, that's great. You won't regret it!"

Darya didn't explain that she had no idea what "good" things she planned to use her wishes on. She didn't explain that she wouldn't know what she would wish for until she figured out the riddle of the Forgetting Spell. That was the key. She just knew it.

She also didn't explain that the one thing she was positive she *wouldn't* wish for was the one thing Mama wanted her to wish for, for Emily to come back.

She didn't explain herself at all, and yet Natasha's expression changed from flummoxed to happy.

Darya had to look away.

"Can I still—just quickly—tell you what Mama wanted you to know?" Natasha asked.

Darya tried to imagine she was behind a waterfall, watching the world from a peaceful place where nothing could hurt her. She'd read that was a good meditation practice.

"When Mama was in the seventh grade, there was a contest, something called an Academic Olympiad, and everyone had to write essays and solve problems and all sorts of stuff. Then came the judging, which was a whole 'nother deal. Anyway, Emily won. Mama was thirteen, and her best friend did better than she did. She was jealous."

The waterfall didn't work. Natasha's words got through regardless, as did the contradiction between reality and make-believe. Because *Mama* had won that contest, the Academic Olympiad, which Darya knew because she'd seen the pictures in the old yearbook. And *Academic Olympiad*, that goofy term. The yearbook was where Darya had heard of it!

"Mama's Wishing Day was the day after the winners were announced, and Mama wished that she'd won instead," Natasha said. "That was her impossible wish."

*Sure, kid, you can win that Academic Olympiad,* Darya imagined a wish fairy whispering to her mother when she was thirteen years old. *Gotta go back in time to make that work, though. And what are we gonna do with the original winner? Can't have two girls winning the contest. One girl, one winner. Winner winner, chicken dinner!*

255

"And then the *next* day, when Mama woke up, Emily was gone."

*Sure*, Darya thought. *Buh-bye, Emily, and thanks for playing. You take care, hear?*

Natasha touched Darya's shoulder. She waited for Darya to focus on her, and then she said, "Emily didn't go *missing*, as if she'd run away or been kidnapped or something. She was just . . . gone, as if she'd never been born. As if she'd never been Papa's little sister, as if she'd never been Mama's best friend. And do you want to know the worst thing?"

"It's *all* the worst thing," Darya mumbled.

"What? I missed that."

Darya pressed her lips together.

"The worst part was Mama was the *only one* who remembered Emily at all."

Goose bumps rippled over Darya's forearms. If a living, breathing human being could disappear on the whim of a jealous thirteen-year-old, the universe made no sense at all.

"But Mama never meant that to happen," Natasha said.

*But it did*, Darya thought.

"She felt horrible."

*So horrible that she went on to marry Papa, Emily's*

*big brother. So awful that they had three daughters:*
*you, me, and Ava, and everyone was happy, until*
*Mama unraveled it all. She abandoned us because of*
*something sad that happened years and years ago, and*
*I'm supposed to say, "Oh, it's so sad, but since she*
*feels* horrible *about it . . ."*

"Darya?" Natasha said.

"Mama was as bad a friend as Tally," Darya muttered.

"What? You're not making sense—and why won't you look at me?"

"I am looking at you."

"No, you're, like . . . looking *through* me. Maybe you should go to your room and rest or something."

"Yes, that sounds good." She headed, robot-like, toward the house.

"Darya, for real, are you okay?"

Darya didn't reply. Then she thought, *What the heck?*

She looked back at Natasha and said, "You know, I'm really not. Do you care?"

"Of course I care! Do *you*? Because I try and I try, but you're so negative about everything!"

Darya felt the heavy weight of despair again, because she didn't *want* to be negative. She was sick of being negative. Natasha could see so many things, so why couldn't she see that?

The hopefulness that had brightened Natasha faded away. Darya watched it happen. "Well, I'm still glad you're going to help Mama."

"I'm glad you're glad," Darya replied.

# CHAPTER TWENTY-FOUR

Alone in her room, Darya opened Mama's letter. She shook out the sheets of paper—there were three of them—and read them:

Darling Darya,

I know you must be mad at me, and I'm sorry.
I know you understand none of this.
I know I've let you down.
I'm so very sorry.
I could tell you I'm sorry all day long, and it wouldn't be enough, would it?

My feisty girl. My redheaded spitfire. There's an old Russian proverb about gingers. Did you know that? For that matter, do you know what a "ginger" is?

Ack. You're thirteen now, not five, and here I am being the sort of parent I promised myself I'd never be. The parent who gives her daughter paper dolls when she'd prefer makeup, or a copy of <u>Black Beauty</u> when she outgrew horse stories when she was eleven.

I'm not thinking of you in particular, Darya. Well, I am. Obviously. But I'm also thinking about Emily, who was my best friend when I was your age. Emily's parents were divorced. Her father didn't live in Willow Hill, and although he loved her, he didn't know her. How could he? He talked to her on the phone. He saw her for two weeks every summer. Sometimes he drove from wherever he lived to Willow Hill and took her and her brother out for dinner.

He was a good man. He tried to be a good father. But to Emily, he felt like "an acquaintance plus." That's how she put it. Not a stranger, but not her dad. Not the way the rest of us had dads.

For Emily's thirteenth birthday, her father gave her a pillow with a rainbow and a unicorn on it. She'd wanted a new set of pastels. She was an artist; she won first place in the Academic Olympiad that year. The

contest covered all disciplines—math, history, English—
but it was a question about freedom of expression that
made her entry stand out. The rest of us wrote essays.
Emily drew a picture, a landscape she called "Lavender
Field and the Milky Way."

It was spectacular.

Oh, Darya. I didn't set out to write about Emily.
Not like this. I'd go back and scratch out every
sentence, except I promised myself I wouldn't, not
again. No more erasing.

Today is your Wishing Day! (If Papa remembered
my instructions, that is. I left him a letter, too. I asked
him to give this to you on your Wishing Day, but
before you made your wishes. Did he?)

I suppose I wanted to give you all sorts of wisdom,
but I'm a bit short of wisdom, I'm afraid. I can barely
make one thought stick to the next these days. For
heaven's sake, I didn't even tell you the proverb about
gingers, did I?

Well, here it is: There never was a saint with red
hair.

Are you blown away?

Didn't think so. On the other hand, who wants to
be a saint, anyway? If you're human, you can't be a
saint. If you're a saint, you're not human. But forget

saints. What I want to tell you about is magic.

There's magic everywhere, I think, but in Willow Hill, magic shimmers in an eternal, invisible mist. Not everyone can sense it, and so not everyone believes in it. On the other hand, if you <u>do</u> sense it, you have no choice but to believe in it.

When you were three, you blew on a dandelion, and the dandelion fluff turned into a swirl of butterflies. Do you remember? You clapped and bounced and said, "Again! Again!" Now, I'd had my suspicions about you since you were a baby. You babbled to no one, but not the way other babies did. You'd gurgle a string of nonsense syllables, and then you'd pause and widen your eyes. Then you'd burst into peals of giggles and babble some more, as if you and whatever tree spirit or water sprite you were talking to were having the most delightful conversation.

But when you blew butterflies out of a dandelion, I knew for sure. Magic runs deep in your veins, Darya. I don't know if it's a blessing or a curse. Probably both.

I gripped your shoulders and gazed into your eyes and told you it had to be our secret. "You can't tell <u>anyone</u>. Not Papa, not your sisters, not your aunts," I said, but I came on too strong. I frightened you and made you think you'd done something bad. I made you doubt yourself.

Don't, Darya. Don't doubt yourself, especially today.

<u>Make your wishes with care</u>.

That's really all I've got—except it would be cowardly of me to leave it at that. You don't want my advice. You want to know why I left, don't you?

I love you.

I will always love you.

And you might not believe me, but I didn't leave because I wanted to. I left because I saw no other choice. Call it a lack of imagination, if you want. That always was a flaw of mine.

Emily, though. Emily had imagination. Emily saw fields of lavender where the rest of us saw weeds. She gave the world tangerine skies; I took those skies away.

Be careful what you wish for, darling Darya.

I love you.

I love you.

I love you.

—Mama

Darya let the pages fall to her lap. Her chest rose and fell, and a gushing wave of missingness crashed over her and tried *so hard* to wash her away. She gripped Mama's letter so tightly that she crumpled it, and then she opened her fingers and choked out a sob.

She gathered the pages, smoothed them as best she could, and refolded them. She slid them back into the envelope and put the envelope into the top drawer of her bedside table.

No, that was no good. Someone had taken it before. She wasn't going to let that happen again.

She tapped the corner of the envelope against her lip. In her closet, way back in the corner, was a shoebox. Inside the shoebox were all the riddles and picture puzzles Mama had given her, as well as any that Darya had drawn for Mama. She rifled through the scraps of paper, drawing several out for a closer examination.

$$\frac{\text{stood}}{\text{MISS}}$$

*Misunderstood.* An easy one, but satisfying. And appropriate.

She studied it, then nodded. *Big fish in a small pond.*

She gave a small smile. It had been a long time since she'd thought about these puzzles. She enjoyed re-figuring them out.

She worked out several more, until she unexpectedly grew light-headed and had to stop. Something about the scraps bothered her, but as with so many things recently, she couldn't put her finger on what.

Still, her box of riddles was where she kept all things Mama, so she tucked Mama's letter among the scraps of paper. She put the lid on the box and placed the box back in her closet.

There. The shoebox was a vault for storing valuables, and there was a word puzzle that described those valuables perfectly:

⟹SECRET
SECRET
SECRET

*I wish I knew how to love Klara better! Klara
and our baby girls. I can't . . . I don't know
how . . . without her, I don't think I could
survive. Oh, please don't let her slip away!*

—Nathaniel Blok, age twenty-five

# CHAPTER TWENTY-FIVE

*(before)*

Darya plays on her big girl bed with the safety railing finally taken off. Mama is playing with her. It's just the two of them, the way Darya likes best.

Mama piles up pillows on the mattress, a hundred of them or at least a dozen. She lifts Darya from under her armpits and plops her onto the tippity-toppiest pillow of them all.

"There!" she proclaims.

Darya wobbles. "I'm going to fall!" she cries.

"Not if you hold still. You're a big girl, Darya. You can do this."

Darya grows solemn, because if Mama says she

can, she can. She *will*. When she stops worrying about falling, she takes in her new view of the world. She's on top of the pillows. The pillows are on top of the bed. The floor holds the bed up, the house holds the floor up, and way way down, the ground holds up the house, which holds up the floor, the bed, the pillows, and high-as-a-princess Darya.

*But what holds the world up?* Darya wonders.

She asks Mama, who smiles and says that's a big question for a little girl.

"Tell me," Darya begs.

"Well, if you must know"—she lowers her voice as if they were spies—"it's a turtle."

"*Mama.*"

"Don't you believe me?"

Darya thinks about the turtle that lives at preschool. His name is Harold. He sits in the glass aquarium and does nothing.

A turtle like Harold couldn't hold up the world, which tells Darya that Mama is teasing.

Darya decides to tease her back. "Okay, then what holds the turtle up?"

Mama laughs, making Darya beam.

"Another turtle!" she'd said. "And another and another and another. It's turtles all the way down!"

"No, it's not!"

"You're right. It's *Daryas* all the way down." She puts her finger on Darya's nose and pushes her— *fwoomph!*—so that she lands on her back. Mama stacks the pillows on top of *her.*

"Don't move," she cautions. "Don't move!"

When Mama is done, a hundred pillows, or at least five, are balanced on Darya's tummy.

"There," says Mama. "Now you're the bottomest turtle, holding everything up. What's it like? Do you feel like you've got the weight of the world on your shoulders?"

"No, on my *tummy.*"

Mama laughs. This makes Darya laugh. This makes the pillows fall, and Mama falls too. *Tink, tink, tink,* like dominoes, with Mama toppling gently and landing with her head on Darya where the pillows used to be.

"I caught you!" Darya exclaims, bolting upright. She keeps her legs straight so that she doesn't dislodge Mama. "Mama, I caught you!"

"You did, you clever girl!"

Darya beams. She loves Mama all the time, but she loves her so so much when she's in a sunshine mood.

"What if I . . . fall off a chair?" Mama asks, gazing

with twinkling upside-down eyes at Darya. "Will you catch me then?"

"Yup."

"What if I fall off a table?"

"Yup."

"What if I fall off a *mountain*? And don't say 'yup,' because I would squish you, little girl!"

Mama rolls over and scrambles onto her knees and tickles Darya with crazy tickling fingers.

"I'll catch you anyway!" Darya cries, laughing like she'll never stop. She doesn't *want* to stop, never not ever. "I'll always catch you!"

"Always?" Mama presses, tickling harder.

"Always! Always!" She laughs and squirms all over the place. "And you can't make me not. So there!"

Mama lifts her hands. Darya is still filled with giggle bubbles, but the relief is exquisite.

"I am the luckiest mama in the world," Mama says.

Darya screeches when Mama pretends to come for her again. "And I'm the luckiest Darya."

# CHAPTER TWENTY-SIX

That night, after sinking into a gray and troubled sleep, Darya woke with a start. She'd had a nightmare filled with tumbling baby blocks decorated with etchings of birds and the ABCs in a fancy font. There'd been a ferocious wind, and the Bird Lady on a bicycle that turned into a broom, like the Wicked Witch of the West. *Da dunh da dunh da* dunh *da. Da dunh da dunh da* dunh *da.*

Then the Bird Lady transformed into Tally, who hovered by Darya's bedroom window cackling and flaunting the letter from Mama. The wind had blown, and the bough had broken, and down had come baby, ABC blocks and all.

"It was a dream," Darya said out loud.

But it was also a message. ABC blocks, Mama's letter, Tally as a wicked witch. Only Tally wasn't a wicked witch. She was just a girl who'd made a bad decision.

What did that say about Mama, who'd made a bad decision as well—and then some? Was Darya supposed to lump Mama and Tally together, both of them just girls who made really bad decisions?

Maybe, and maybe, one day, she could forgive them. If she decided to.

If, if, if! So many ifs! Pull on any one of them, and everything could unravel.

If Mama hadn't erased Emily (a bad thing), then there would be no Darya. Maybe Mama and Papa would have still gotten married, and maybe they'd still have had three little girls. But no way would each second tick out in precisely the pattern needed to ensure that the middle child was Darya and not some random fake child. Dora or Daria or . . . *Siobhan*, for heaven's sake.

Likewise, if Tally hadn't stolen Mama's letter (a bad thing), then Darya wouldn't have run into the Bird Lady and gotten a hint about the Forgetting Spell. Not that the hint had gotten her anywhere.

But maybe, in this thorny world Darya lived in, "thinking outside the box" was the only way forward, about good and bad, right and wrong? About life, the universe, and everything?

Darya's eyes widened, while everything else—her thoughts, her cells, the tiny hairs on the back of her neck—narrowed to a pinprick of white hot concentration.

*Think outside the box.*

*Think outside the* box.

The *box*! Of course! Not a metaphorical "let's learn a lesson" box, but a real box. Her box. Her box of puzzles and riddles!

She scrambled out of bed, dashed to her closet, and pulled out the shoebox. She flung off the lid and sifted through the scraps of paper. Which one was the answer? Which one would set free her forgotten memories?

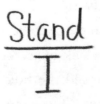

"I understand," Darya whispered, barely giving breath to the words.

*No, I don't,* she thought, tossing that one aside. *I want to, but I'm not there yet.*

She went through half a dozen more. Some were clever, some were a little dumb, although she reminded herself that she'd been little when she and Mama had solved these puzzles together.

Some made her smile, like the one that showed a soup tin, among other things.

*Can you see I love you?* she thought. *I don't know. Can I?*

Others stumped her for several minutes. For example, a riddle scribbled onto a ripped-off piece of paper that said, "If I have it, I don't share it. If I share it, I don't have it. What is it?"

Then the solution came to her—a secret. The thing was, she was getting sick of secrets.

At last she upturned the box and dumped all the scraps onto the carpet. One scrap remained even when she shook it. Darya examined it more closely, running her thumbnail under the edge. It was glued in place so that it couldn't come out.

It was an easy one:

# THINK

*Yeah, I know,* she thought. *I'm trying!*

And, like a lock sliding home, it came to her, because sometimes—omigosh—a box is just a box. The answer had been there all the time!

She checked the outside edges of the shoebox. Nothing, just the word "Adidas." She flipped the box over, and there it was. A scrap of paper glued to the cardboard that said, "When is a door not a door?"

"When is a door not a door?"

She knew this one. Everyone knew this one. *When is a door not a door? When it's ajar, of course.*

With that, the door to Darya's subconscious was knocked ajar, and a memory rushed in:

*"Mama, where are you going?"*

*"Just . . . away, baby."*

*"Why?"*

*"Because I have to."*

*"When will you be back? Can I come too?"*

*"I don't know, and no. Let go of my leg now. Mama's got to leave."*

*"No, I don't want you to!"*

*"Darya, let go."*

*"Mama, please!"*

*"Let go, Darya."*

*There was urgency and the need to pee. Swirls of confusion. Everything was wrong, and Mama was going to leave—unless Darya stopped her.*

*Darya had to stop her.*

*"If I ask you a riddle—"*

*"I don't have time for riddles, baby. I'm sorry."*

*"You interrupted! If I ask you a riddle and you don't get it, then will you stay?"*

*"Darya . . ."*

*"Please! Please!"*

*A sigh. "Fine. Go ahead, then."*

*Hope, bursting in her lungs. Think! Think, think, think!*

*Then . . . yes!*

*"When is a door not a door?"*

*"Oh, Darya." (So sad. Don't use that sad voice. No!) "When it's ajar. Now let me go, sweetheart."*

*"Mama, no!"*

*Hands prying at hands. Clutching. Falling. Getting up and running.*

*"Mama! Mama!"*

*And then . . . g plus one, gone.*

*It's Darya's fault.*

*It will always be Darya's fault.*

*Forever.*

Grief brought her back. Grief and the taste of salt, as she sat on the floor by the upside-down shoebox, tears streaming down her cheeks.

She had been so certain that remembering what she'd forgotten would make things better, but it hadn't.

How could she fix things?

She couldn't. That was the answer she'd been hiding from, both horrible and true. She knew from the way it hit home, the way the right answers always did.

# CHAPTER TWENTY-SEVEN

She waited, trapped between remembering and for-getting, until the sun sent its watery yellow rays through her curtains.

A *jar*, she'd thought when she was little. How embarrassing. A door, a jar, a jar of fireflies. A jar of memories that had finally leaked out.

But the sun was up. Dawn had arrived. It was October thirtieth, which for everyone else meant the day before Halloween. For Darya, it was her Wishing Day at last.

She stood up, wiped her eyes, and slipped down-stairs, where she pulled her jacket over her pajama top and shoved her feet into her boots, letting the legs of her PJ bottoms bunch up as they chose.

*Make your wishes with care*, Mama had warned in her letter, and Darya would.

As she hiked to the top of Willow Hill, she shivered at the thought of all that could go wrong. Still, she kept going. She was Darya Blok, and magic ran in her veins. She was *not* a quitter.

From the top of the hill, she surveyed the town. Was Mama asleep in the charming garage apartment she shared with Aunt Elena? Or was she awake, possibly thinking about Darya? A jolt of fear electrified her. Mama wasn't *here*, was she? Lying in wait to force Darya to do as she bid?

A hasty scan of the clearing told her that no, Mama wasn't here. Darya was alone, the wind whipping her hair. She felt like a warrior. She felt like a princess. She felt like a stupid teenage girl, wearing a nightshirt and an army jacket.

She approached the ancient willow tree. Its branches swayed and murmured. Darya ducked her head and pushed through the frost-covered fronds.

She laid her palm against the willow's trunk and bright white energy buzzed around her, zapping her skin and tousling her hair. *It's like when I hold my breath, but not,* she thought.

Darya sensed an invisible precipice—*here there be wishes*—and she stepped off willingly.

*A Girl, Falling.*

"Number one, my impossible wish," Darya said. "I wish to know what happened—what *really* happened—to Emily." She couldn't and wouldn't "wish Emily back." Too dangerous. But the truth about Emily? Yes, please. Darya would like very much to solve that riddle, even though the chance of that happening seemed very small.

"For the wish I can make come true myself . . ." She hesitated, and the bark of the willow tree rippled under her fingers. She pressed her hand against the trunk and made her entire body tight and unyielding. "I wish to have nothing to do with Mama."

Wind moaned in the willow's long fronds. Darya held steady against it. She couldn't save Mama when she was little, and she couldn't save her now.

"And my third wish. The deepest wish of my secret heart." Her voice wavered, because she didn't *know* the deepest wish of her secret heart! If life was fair, then Tally would have this wish, because Tally would do the right thing and wish something good, something that had to do with her mother. Darya almost made that her wish, that Tally could have *her* heart's desire, until a stab of resentment poisoned the impulse.

*You have* so *much*, Tally had said, as if that made her betrayal okay. *You have no idea how lucky you are.*

Maybe, but Tally had no idea how lucky she was, either. Like with her art, and how talented she was. Darya could . . . she could wish to be even more talented than Tally! That would show her!

Something shuddered through Darya. She whirled around, but saw nothing except for the swaying, frost-laden branches of the willow.

*And* down *will come* bay-*bee* . . .

But no, nobody had to come down, and she would not use her final wish that way, whether the ritual was real *or* make-believe. That's what Mama had done. Darya refused to follow in her footsteps.

"I wish Papa would be happy again," she said in a rush, and there, see? She did wish that, and she'd been unselfish, and . . . it was done.

*It was done.*

She pushed through the willow's canopy of branches and stepped back into the real world. A breeze made goose pimples raise on her flesh, but other than that, she felt like the same old Darya.

Well, what else did she expect?

Back at the house, she took off her boots and tiptoed upstairs, planning to turn around when she reached the top and clatter back down. She could get breakfast started as a surprise for Aunt Vera. She could continue to be unselfish. She could turn over a new leaf.

But she was so drowsy. Impossibly drowsy.

She climbed into her bed and nestled under the covers, intending to take a power nap. The next thing she knew, an enormous owl grabbed her with its talons. The owl soared up, and Darya found herself on top of the owl's broad back, holding tight to its feathers and clamping her thighs around its huge warm body.

The owl became a car. Darya was the driver. The steering wheel spun loosely, and the road came at her with whips and curves and then the steepest hill she could ever imagine. A roller-coaster hill that the car relentlessly climbed, *crick crick crick*. And then the road ended, and the car kept going, soaring into . . . nothing.

And yet, as she floated through silence, she wasn't gripped by terror. Instead, she felt bubble-wrapped in safety.

*Let go*, her dream self told her. *Everything's going to work out.*

Someone rapped on her door, and she woke up.

"Yeah?" she said.

"It's your Wishing Day!" Ava crowed, bursting into the room. She hip-hopped to Darya's bed and dropped onto the mattress. She bounced Darya up and down. "Aren't you excited? Aren't you so so SO excited?!"

"No," Darya said.

"Yes you are. Don't say that." Ava punched Darya in the shoulder, then stopped bouncing. She peered at Darya, taking Darya's face in her hands and turning her this way and that. "Something's different about you. What'd you do?"

"Nothing," Darya said.

Ava stroked Darya's cheek.

Darya swatted her away.

"What? I can't touch you now?"

"You can touch me. Just, stop being weird."

Ava made a *whatever* gesture. "*Any*way, Natasha and I think we should go with you to the willow tree instead of the aunts. Do you want to go now or after breakfast? Or would you rather go tonight?"

"Um . . . I've already gone."

"You already *went*? By yourself? Did you make your wishes?"

Darya's heart constricted at Ava's need to double-check that not only did Darya go to the willow tree by herself, but that yes, she remembered to make her wishes when she was there.

She flung back her covers to show Ava her pajamas, socks, and army jacket.

"Oh," Ava said. She glanced at Darya as if for permission. Darya sighed, then nodded. Ava ran her finger over the vine on Darya's jacket. "It was cold, huh? You must have been up early."

Darya could see her sister framing her next question. She answered before Ava could speak.

"I'm not telling you, Ava."

"Right," Ava said, blushing. She scanned Darya's room. "Well, you didn't wish for a pony, or we'd see it."

"Because the pony would be in my bedroom?"

Ava furrowed her brow. She hopped off the bed and went to the window, and Darya half smiled.

Natasha appeared in the doorway. "Happy Wishing Day."

"Thanks."

Ava filled Natasha in about how Darya had already made her wishes. Natasha listened and nodded. She studied Darya in a way that made Darya want to pull the covers over her head. Natasha wasn't going to try to touch Darya too, was she?

Darya kicked the covers all the way off, stood up,

and herded her sisters out of her room.

At her dresser, she leaned forward, examining her reflection in the attached mirror. Clear skin, curly hair, the same unruly cowlick as always, a thick lock of hair that refused to lie the right way. She looked good. Not great, not horrible, but good. *Normal.*

The only real difference was that she was wearing her army jacket over her pajamas. The shirt part was white and soft and had a picture of a kitten on it, and there was something . . . interesting about the contrast between squishy adorable cute and army jacket tough.

*Hmm.*

She decided to switch out her PJ bottoms for jeans (duh), but to keep on her PJ top and let that be her shirt for the day (after wiggling into a bra). (Duh.) She left her hair bedhead messy and didn't attempt to tame her cowlick. When she gave herself a final glance in the mirror, she liked what she saw. She felt kind of cool.

She felt cool for the entire day, strangely enough. It was some sort of fluke, obviously. But she *deserved* a fluke, she decided. She'd take what she could.

# CHAPTER TWENTY-EIGHT

Friday was Halloween, and at Willow Hill Middle School, kids were allowed to celebrate Halloween by going to school in costume, as long as there weren't guns, knives, or gore involved, or skirts that left too little to the imagination.

Darya decided to go as herself, but gypsy-style. A wild girl, striding through life with her wishes behind her and the future hers to claim. She wore a flowy skirt, a cream-colored peasant blouse, and a gauzy scarf from Ava. Dangly earrings that chimed when she moved. Sandals to show off cherry-red toenails, despite the chilly weather, because gypsies and bare feet went together like jam and toast. To top it off, her army jacket.

She gave herself a once-over in her mirror, noting that again, she looked kind of . . . good. She adjusted a curl, and there. Done.

On the way to school, two middle-aged mom-types complimented her costume, one of them saying to the other, "Now that is a cute outfit. Cute *and* hip. We were never that hip, were we, Doris?"

"Never," Doris said. She smiled at Darya, then made a surprised O with her mouth. "You're Nate Blok's daughter, aren't you?"

"Um . . . yeah?" Darya said. Outside of their family, people called Papa "Nathaniel," not Nate. She put on a friendly face and crinkled her nose to say, *And you are . . . ?*

"Oh, I'm Angela's friend," the Doris lady said. "*So* nice to meet you!"

*Well, that clears it up*, Darya thought. *Who's Angela?* She looked at the other woman. Was she Angela?

"I'm Nina," the woman said, offering her hand. Darya shook it, but shaking hands with grown-ups was weird, she decided.

"Tell your dad hi from us!" Doris said.

"Okay, I will!" Darya replied.

"Have a great day!"

"You, too!"

*Weird*, she thought again when the women moved along.

School was fine. Her friends were fine. They asked questions about her Wishing Day, but they knew better than to push overly hard. Anyway, it was Halloween.

Steph had dressed up as a princess. Her blond hair cascaded in complicated twists and braids down her back. Her skin glowed. Her lips, as red as Darya's toenails, formed a perfect lush bow. When she spotted Darya, her eyes lit up and sparkled and did all of the shiny, marvelous things eyes should do.

*That* was magic, Darya thought.

Suki was an emoji, or maybe an anime girl with big anime eyes. She looked adorable.

Tally was absent.

Darya had geared herself up for seeing her—might as well get it over with, she'd told herself—but it turned out she didn't have to. Great. Terrific. Only, where was she?

After third period, when she should have seen Tally in the art room, Darya found Suki and dragged her into an empty classroom.

"Do you know where Tally is?" she said.

Suki's eyes widened. She kept her gaze firmly on Darya's, but maintaining eye contact at all costs was actually Suki's tell. When Suki glanced here, there, and everywhere, that was Suki being Suki. When Suki looked straight at you, she was saying, *Look! I'm looking straight at you! I'm not hiding anything, no way!*

"She's sick?" Suki said.

*What is Suki hiding?* Darya wondered. "Bummer. With what?"

"The flu?"

"Wow, poor Tally. I hung out with her on Wednesday, and she was fine."

"It came on quick."

"Yeah, that happens. What did she not want you to tell me?"

"That her mom might be coming to visit! Isn't that awesome?"

"Huh," Darya said.

Suki clapped her hand over her mouth. "I didn't say that. I really didn't!"

"Why didn't she want you to tell me?"

Suki squirmed.

"*Suki* . . ."

291

"She thinks you're mad at her. She . . . didn't want you to be jealous."

"Well, I'm not," Darya said, not knowing how she felt. "But, so what. She stayed home in order to see her?"

"She skipped. She didn't want to miss her mom's call, *if* she called." Suki frowned. "It was kind of random, actually. Like, why all of a sudden? And couldn't her mom text?"

It broke Darya's heart a little. *Couldn't Tally's mom just text?* Sure, in Suki's world. In Tally's world, things weren't as straightforward. In Darya's world, even less so. Darya didn't even have a cell phone.

"Maybe she didn't want to get busted for using her phone at school," Darya said. "I mean, *teachers*. Am I right?"

Suki tilted her head.

"I think that's awesome, about Tally's mom. Tell her that for me, will you?" She squeezed Suki's shoulder. "When she gets better, I mean."

⌒

That evening, Darya went trick-or-treating with Ava—just to be a good big sister, of course. Strangers filled their pillowcases to the brim with fun-size Snickers and baby Kit Kats and miniature Reese's Cups.

When they returned home, Papa had a treat for them as well. Or maybe a trick, as his gifts gave Darya a funny feeling. He gave both Ava and Darya a slim silver cuff bracelet, each with a different word or saying stamped into it. Ava's said "Dreamer." Darya's said "Stay True."

"Thanks, Papa!" Ava said, flinging herself at him and hugging him. "Did Angela make them? They look like the ones Angela makes. Did you give Natasha one, too? What does hers say?"

"Angela?" Darya said.

"Papa's friend from the art festival," Ava said. "I told you."

Papa turned red. "She hoped you girls might like them. *I* hope you like them."

Darya had no words. She seriously had no words. Was Papa *blushing*?!

Papa cleared his throat. "And, ah, Natasha's says 'Wisdom.'"

Ava slipped hers on. "It fits! It's actually small enough to fit my wrist!"

"I told her what a hard time we've had, finding bracelets that don't slip off you," Papa said.

Darya found her voice. "No, we haven't."

"Yes, we have," Ava said, looking at her funny.

"Really? Just how often have you and Papa gone *bracelet* shopping, and where was I all those times?" She felt a tumble of emotions. "And why does Natasha's say 'Wisdom,' but mine says 'Stay True'? Stay true to what?"

"Angela, I told her about all three of you girls, she picked them out," Papa said.

"Well, fantastic," Darya said. "Did Doris help? And Nina?"

Papa retreated into his shell. "I don't know Doris and Nina. I'm going back to my studio. I've got some work to finish."

"Thanks for the bracelet, Papa!" Ava said. "And tell Angela thanks."

She elbowed Darya.

"Thanks, Papa," she said. She wiggled the bracelet onto her wrist, then promptly wiggled it off once Papa left and gave it to Ava. "Here, now you have two bracelets small enough to actually fit."

"You don't want yours?" Ava said. "Angela's not . . . there's nothing wrong with her."

"Never said there was."

"She's Papa's friend, that's all. If you were thinking anything different."

"I wasn't. Were you?"

294

"Not until now!" Ava fidgeted. "No. She's his friend, and that's all, and I'm glad he has her—but not in that way." She stomped her foot. "You're making things weird. Don't you want Papa to be happy?"

Darya's stomach flipped. Of course she wanted Papa to be happy.

"You've met this Angela person. I haven't. So sure, I'll go with whatever you say." She tossed the bracelet, and Ava caught it. "You can stay true for both of us."

# CHAPTER TWENTY-NINE

Thursday was Darya's Wishing Day, Friday was Halloween, and Saturday, November first, it was Natasha's birthday. The days felt crowded, *bam bam bam*.

"Crap, I forgot to get you a present!" Darya said over breakfast. She, Natasha, and Ava sat at the table by themselves. Aunt Vera was upstairs, and Papa was in his workshop.

"Don't worry about it," Natasha said, waving her hand. "There's been a lot going on."

"Yeah, but—"

"Maybe you *did* give me a present, and you just

don't know it. Or maybe it's invisible." She gave Darya a cryptic look and took a bite of her muffin.

"No," Darya said. "Sorry . . . but no."

Natasha chewed and swallowed. She looked at Darya probingly. "You didn't make a wish about Mama? You didn't make a wish about Emily?"

Darya felt like growling.

"If you say so," Natasha said. "Anyway, I don't need presents. It's all good." Natasha took another bite of muffin, and something shiny caught the light. A silver cuff bracelet, reminding Natasha of all the wisdom she possessed.

"Hey, we're stair steps again," Ava said. She was referring to the fact that for four and a half months, Natasha, Darya, and Ava would each be one year older than the next: Natasha, fourteen; Darya, thirteen; Ava, twelve.

In March, Ava would turn thirteen, and Ava's and Darya's ages would overlap.

On the third day of the third month of *Ava's* thirteenth year . . .

The world was moving forward. It would always be moving forward, and before long, Ava would have *her* Wishing Day. Poor Ava.

After breakfast, Natasha pulled Darya aside.

"Later I'm meeting Mama at Little Bird Bakery. Do you want to come?"

"No thanks," Darya said.

"Ava's going to join us. So is Aunt Elena."

Darya tightened inside. "No thanks," she said again.

Natasha sighed. "Mama was afraid you were going to be like this. Well . . . she says hi, and that she hopes you'll come see her soon."

*I wish Nathaniel would see me, really see me, the way I see him.*

—ANGELA BROWN, AGE THIRTY-NINE

# CHAPTER THIRTY

After a week's absence, Tally came back to school. Darya found her in the art room, sitting on a stool at the drafting table. Her head was bowed, and she was concentrating on her drawing.

"Finally," she said, dropping onto the stool beside her. "Where have you been?"

"Sick," Tally said. She smiled, but it wasn't her normal smile. "The flu."

"I don't think so."

"Think whatever you want," Tally said. She returned to her project, a sketch of a mother and daughter, holding hands. Or Darya assumed it was a mother and a daughter. The mother had long hair and a sad smile. The daughter looked a little like a much younger Tally.

"I'd rather think the truth," Darya said. "How about you tell me that?"

Tally didn't speak for a while. Then she said, "Fine. Yes, I saw my mom."

The world split in two. There was Darya in the art room, and there was Darya on her Wishing Day, alone at the top of Willow Hill. *The deepest wish of my secret heart . . .*

She'd considered giving Tally her wish, knowing that Tally would wish for something good, something that had to do with her mother.

But she hadn't.

And yet.

Darya grabbed a pencil and a piece of paper and dashed off a drawing of a mason jar filled with daisies. It looked like an illustration for a "Deepest Sympathies" card, only more generic.

"That's awesome," she managed.

"You sound jealous," Tally said. "Truth: Are you jealous?"

Darya gestured at Tally's drawing. "Is that, like, the two of you?"

"Is that a yes?"

Ms. Braswell, an English teacher, entered the classroom, followed by several members of the literary magazine. Suki, who was the poetry editor, grinned and waved.

"Darya, Tally! Hello!" Ms. Braswell said. Tally hunched forward to hide her drawing, but she was too late. Ms. Braswell gasped and held it aloft.

Darya and Tally stared at each other. Darya looked away first.

"Tally, this is extraordinary. Clean, simple, and without a pencil mark wasted." She clearly didn't see how uncomfortable Tally was. "Something like this would be perfect for the lit mag's cover illustration."

"Or you could use Darya's," Tally blurted. "It's of flowers."

Darya shot her a look.

"What? Everyone likes flowers."

"Yes, and Darya, your picture is lovely," Ms. Braswell said after giving it the briefest of looks. "But Tally, yours communicates such *emotion*."

"But . . . it's not . . . I didn't do it for . . ." Darya

followed Tally's gaze to something under the table and understood. Tally had a photo balanced on her thigh, a photo of a mom and a little girl. The image Tally was drawing was the image captured in the photo.

"It's personal," Darya blurted.

"It's personal?" Suki said, bouncing over. "How's it personal?" She glanced from Tally's drawing to Tally and back again. "*Ohhh*, is that you and your mom?"

"What? No!"

Darya saw Tally slide the photograph off her leg, hiding it with her hand as best she could. Tally lowered her hand to her side and dropped the photo into her backpack.

Ms. Braswell must have assessed the situation and drawn her own conclusions, because she gave Tally back her drawing. "Well, Tally, I hope you'll consider letting us use this for the literary magazine, but it's up to you."

She led Suki and the other lit mag students to another part of the room, where they fell into a discussion of color versus black-and-white for some other image they planned to use.

"'It's personal'?" Tally hissed. "Thanks a lot."

"I'm sorry," Darya said. "I didn't mean to. But to be fair . . . you started it."

"Did I?"

"You've been absent forever, you didn't return my calls, and just now you were all, 'Oh, are you jealous? You're jealous, aren't you?' That's why Ms. Braswell was able to sneak up on you."

Tally gaped at Darya, and Darya flushed, hearing for herself how petty she sounded.

Tally snapped her mouth shut. Keeping her eyes on Darya's, she ripped her drawing in half, then in half again.

"Tally!" Darya cried in a whisper.

"It's no big deal. I can always draw another." She jerked her chin at Darya's flowers. "You, on the other hand. Guess you didn't mean it when you said you wished you were an artist, huh?"

"Huh?"

Darya looked at her crappy drawing and connected the dots. She obviously hadn't used one of her Wishing Day wishes on being an artist, Tally meant. Or, if she had, the wish hadn't worked.

"Tally, that's mean," she whispered.

Tally puffed up, then deflated. Her eyes welled with tears, and she hopped off the stool and rushed to the front of the room, where she dumped her shredded drawing into the trash can. She grabbed a Kleenex from Ms. Braswell's desk and pressed it to her eyes. She blew her nose.

Darya dropped her gaze to the photo in Tally's backpack. There was writing on the back. —*d Tally, Pop Pop's farm*, she made out. She nudged the backpack with her toe, knocking the photo forward and revealing the hidden words.

Darya grew hot, and once again the world tilted.

Tally came back. She zipped up her backpack and slung it over her shoulder. With what felt like an actual jolt, Darya was thrown forward into the moment, and she heard Tally saying, ". . . but you're right, and I'm sorry." She sniffed. "We're both being stupid. Can we just start fresh?"

"Uh-huh," she said dumbly.

____ *and Tally, Pop Pop's farm*, she'd read on the back of Tally's photo. Then she'd knocked the picture forward, and she'd filled in the blank.

It was a common enough name. Not Tally—Tally was unusual. But the other name was as common as Sarah or Anne or Karen. There were thousands of Sarahs and Annes and Karens in the world, surely. Hundreds of thousands!

Still, what was the line from that old movie? *Of*

*all the gin joints in all the towns in all the world, she walked into mine?* Something like that.

And of all the names in all the world, Tally's mother just had to be named Emily.

# CHAPTER THIRTY-ONE

No matter what Darya did, magic perched like a fat cat on her shoulder. Or, more aptly, like a skinny cat. A wrinkly, hairless Sphynx with accusing eyes and enormous ears.

Darya read an article about Sphynx cats once. People who loved them said they were loyal and affectionate, picking one human to bond with and staying true to that human forever. "Lap Velcro," the writer of the article dubbed them, claiming that once one latched onto you, it wouldn't let go.

But the article said that Sphynxes had a dark side too. They nipped you when they wanted your attention.

Their claws were like little hands, which was *creepy*, and once they were settled on your lap, they were likely to gouge your thighs if you tried to dislodge them.

And, though it didn't happen often, a Sphynx *could* turn on its owner, the article claimed. A middle-aged woman was slashed across the face by her Sphynx, and not even plastic surgery could mask the scar. A baby in Tennessee lost an eye.

If Darya could choose, which would she pick: Wishing Day magic or a furless cat who could turn evil on the flip of a coin?

But she *couldn't* choose. That was the point. Or, maybe, she *did* choose, and that was the point. Darya had made those wishes up by the ancient willow, after all. No one had held a gun to her head.

ALTHOUGH DARYA HADN'T MADE ANY-ONE DISAPPEAR!

That was big. That was *huge*. She comforted herself with that knowledge when she returned to the art room after school let out and gathered the four jagged pieces of Tally's sketch. She taped them together and studied the woman's face. *Emily's* face.

*No, no, no*, she told herself. *Unless . . . unless unless?*

Several evenings later, when Papa's friend, Angela,

joined them for dinner, Darya reminded herself again that even if she'd somehow conjured this overly smiley woman into Papa's life (unlikely . . . unless unless unless), at least she hadn't erased someone.

Papa smiled at Angela, and a hole of loneliness opened in her heart.

*What have I done?* she wondered.

On the day after Thanksgiving, Darya was thrown a bone. Not a turkey bone, but a symbolic bone. A sister bone. Two sister bones, actually. One from Natasha and one from Ava.

The three sisters had stuffed themselves on leftovers and were sprawled in the den watching *The Wizard of Oz*, which they all still enjoyed. Aunt Vera had gone into town, and Papa was in his workshop. Aunt Elena was at her own apartment, presumably with Mama.

Natasha had on nice jeans and a soft pink sweater. Darya peered closer and saw that she was even wearing lip gloss and mascara, which was unusual for Natasha. Ava was stretched out on the floor in polka-dot leggings, a flippy purple skirt, and a long-sleeved shirt. Darya had on sweats and a tank top. More and more, she was becoming the sloppy sister.

"Hey, Darya?" Natasha said.

"Yeah?" Darya said.

"You've got to tell Papa not to . . . date . . . Angela."

Darya's heart skipped a beat. "Excuse me?"

"She's flirting with him—didn't you see the way she was at dinner?—and it's disgusting."

"Wait, what?" Darya sat up straighter. "I thought you liked Angela. You said she was Papa's friend, and that you wanted Papa to be . . . you know. Happy."

"I do want him to be happy," Natasha said. "But she's taking it too far, don't you think?"

"Yes! I do, totally!"

"Plus she's *old*," Ava said.

"She is?" Darya asked.

"She's going to be forty. I heard her talking about it."

"Papa's thirty-seven. That's only three years—" Darya broke off. Angela was *not* for Papa, not in that way. There was no point discussing her age.

Ava rolled onto her side and looked up at her. "And omigosh, won't you please come with us to see Mama? Whatever you did or didn't wish for, she's not mad. She just misses you."

"Well, I don't miss her," Darya answered, although she did.

"It seems like you're being stubborn over nothing," Ava said.

*Fair enough*, Darya thought, because maybe she was. "What made you decide all of a sudden to tell me this?" she asked. "And why do I have to be the one to tell Papa not to . . ." Nope, she couldn't say it. "Why do I have to tell him that Angela can only be a friend?"

Natasha and Ava shared a look.

"*What?*" Darya pressed.

"Because you're better at being honest," Natasha said.

"What?!" Darya said. She was not! She was better at being *dis*honest, at least if dishonest meant keeping secrets.

*Oh, wow*, she thought, her smile falling away. *I did this to myself, didn't I?* The wishes she'd made—about Mama, about Papa, and about Emily—made her see things where possibly there was nothing to see, which made her keep secrets when possibly there was nothing secret going on at all. Being so suspicious of everyone had made her retreat inside herself, leaving her feeling like . . . like a sleep-deprived ghost!

She couldn't blame her sisters or family or friends for how alone she felt. She could only blame herself. *Mama "disappeared" Emily*, she thought. *By pulling away from everyone who cares about me, I "disappeared" myself.*

"Also, the Angela thing didn't start until after your Wishing Day," Ava said.

"Huh?" Darya said.

"You asked why you have to tell Papa to back off, and we're telling you," Ava said. She and Natasha shared another look. "I mean, maybe the Angela thing is because of you or maybe it's not. You tell us."

"It wasn't!" Darya laughed uneasily. "Well . . . it might have been. But I really doubt it."

"We know," Ava said.

On TV, Dorothy and the Scarecrow had joined forces with the Tin Man, and the three of them were entering the woods. Soon they'd run into the Cowardly Lion.

*Lions and tigers and bears, oh my!*

Darya grabbed the remote and hit the Mute button. "Do you still love me?" she asked in a small voice.

"Darya! Always!" Ava said.

Darya turned to Natasha. "Do you still *like* me?"

"Of course," Natasha said after only a moment's hesitation. "Some times more than others, but that's normal."

"I guess."

"Come with us to Aunt Elena's apartment for cookies and hot chocolate," Ava urged.

"Please?" Natasha said. "If you want us to like you . . . that would definitely help."

"Natasha," Ava scolded.

"No, she's just telling the truth," Darya said. A weight dropped down on her, because she still felt tricked. It was unfair that she should have to pay the price of disappointing Mama. It was unfair that she should have to talk to Papa about . . . Angela.

She shuddered.

It was unfair that she, and only she, knew about the taped-together picture of Tally's mother, which she'd hidden in the puzzle box in her closet.

She swallowed and circled around to what she could say aloud. "Mama shouldn't have asked me to wish for Emily to come back," she said. "That wasn't fair."

"I agree," Ava said.

"You do?"

"Well, I can see both sides of it," Ava said. "But that's in the past now. It's time to move on."

Darya fumbled for a retort, then regrouped and said, "I don't know if I can. And if you understand the unfairness of how Mama acted, then you should understand that."

"And *you* should understand that you have to get

over yourself," countered Natasha.

Darya aimed the remote at the TV and turned the sound back on. Dorothy and the others had arrived at the Emerald City, but the doorman was trying to keep them out.

"State your business!" he said.

"We want to see the Wizard," Dorothy said.

Natasha stood and angled herself in Darya's line of view. "Darya, come with us."

*I can't,* Darya answered silently and miserably. *I'm trying, but I'm not there yet.*

Natasha whirled around all at once. "Come on, Ava. Let's go."

Ava followed Natasha out of the den, and a few seconds later, Darya heard them leave through the back door. The house was silent except for the "ha ha ha"s and "ho ho ho"s from the residents of the Emerald City. Dorothy and the others had gotten in, but they still hadn't seen the Wizard. Even when they *did* see him, he wasn't going to give them what they asked for.

*I wish I could make my wishes now.*

—AVA BLOK, AGE TWELVE AND A HALF

# CHAPTER THIRTY-TWO

Darya clicked off the TV. What was the point when the entire movie was a trick? *Silly Dorothy, you never had to go to Oz at all. You just had to click your ruby slippers, and voilà! Your problems would be solved!*

As if the answer was so obvious, once Dorothy knew it. But it wasn't! Who went around clicking the heels of her ruby slippers? And why *one-two-three* and *close your eyes* and the fervent "I want to go home" incantation? The solution couldn't be both "magic" *and* "there all along." It had to be one or the other.

She trudged upstairs and threw herself onto her

bed, resting her cheek on her forearms and letting her feet hang off the mattress. Then she curled up on her side, drawing her knees to her chest.

She grew cold, but she was too stubborn to crawl under the covers. Or maybe she refused to crawl under the covers because she wanted to punish herself. Or test herself. She didn't know.

The clock on her dresser ticked.

Minutes passed, then an hour. She dozed off, woke up, dozed off again. Outside, the shadows grew long. Inside, everything turned shades of gray.

Darya didn't register the footsteps until they paused outside her room. There was a gentle tap on her door. Groggily, she lifted her head.

"Aunt Vera?" she said.

The doorknob turned.

Darya sat up. "Papa?"

The door opened, and a sliver of light outlined a familiar figure.

"It's me," Mama said. "May I please come in?"

Several things happened at once. Tears flooded Darya's eyes, blurring her vision. Because of her blurry vision, and because there was basically a *stranger* in her room, fear kicked in, driving adrenaline through her body.

She scrambled backward, pressing her spine against the headboard of her bed.

"You're not supposed to be here!" She pointed a shaky finger toward the door. "Leave!"

"Darya, baby," Mama said. She patted the air with her palms, a *calm down* gesture that had the opposite effect.

"I'm *not* your baby, and this isn't your house!"

"Darling, this *is* my house. I lived here before you did."

"And then you left. You don't get to come waltzing back."

"I'm hardly waltzing." She stepped forward.

Darya strained to see into the hallway. "Natasha? Ava?"

"It's just me," Mama said.

"Aunt Vera! Aunt Elena!"

"We're the only ones."

What if Mama was here because she was angry? What if Natasha, the good daughter, had used her wishes wisely, but Mama knew that Darya hadn't?

Darya opened her mouth to call for Papa—he would protect her! Then she clamped her mouth shut. Her fear receded, and blind fury rushed to fill the space. Fury at herself, because she was protecting Papa, not the other way around. Fury at Papa for needing protection. Fury at her sisters and Aunt Elena for tricking her by sending Mama to the house, and fury at Mama for creating this whole stupid mess in the first place.

It was dark, and growing darker.

She stretched sideways and turned on her bedside lamp. She kept her gaze trained on Mama, who blinked in the sudden light.

Darya's hand fell to her lap. Her entire body went boneless.

"I guess you can sit down," she said.

Mama stepped toward the bed. She wore brown leather ankle boots with crisscross straps on the front and zippers up the back.

"Those boots will get ruined when it snows," she said.

Mama glanced at her boots. "I suppose they might."

"They *will*."

"Then I won't wear them in the snow," Mama said. She began to lower herself, but Darya said, "Too close. Sit at the very end."

Mama moved several feet back and sat on the edge of the bed.

Darya waited to hear all the ways that she'd let Mama down. She hadn't wished for Emily to come back. That was the big one. What other mistakes might Mama point out?

"Your hair has gotten redder," Mama commented.

"No, it hasn't."

"It has, actually."

"Uh, no. It's *my* hair, you know."

Mama sighed.

"This is nuts, it really is," Darya said. She dared herself to go on. "Are *you* nuts? Is that what I should tell my friends, that I have a crazy person for a mother? Is that what I should tell Papa and Aunt Vera?"

Mama flinched.

"It's fine if you are," Darya said. She fluttered her fingers through the air. "I mean, I might be, too, so who am I to judge?"

"You're not crazy," Mama said.

"Then what am I?" Darya said.

"A girl," Mama said. "A beautiful, brave, intelligent thirteen-year-old girl who made three foolish wishes, from what I can gather."

Darya had known it was coming. She'd known it, and it still hurt.

"You're not crazy, but you *are* like me," Mama continued. "I warned you to be careful what you wished for!"

"How do you know I wasn't?"

"Then why is Nate seeing this . . . this *Angela* I keep hearing about?"

"Maybe because he wants to. Maybe because he's lonely. Maybe—oh, newsflash—because *you* left him."

Mama's lips tightened. "And Emily?"

Darya's pulse spiked. The picture Tally had drawn was a good likeness. Darya could show Mama right now and get an answer to the question—her own question—once and for all.

"You didn't wish her back," Mama stated.

"Ava said you didn't care," Darya retorted.

"We need to talk about it, just you and me." She lifted her chin. "I'll live, but I *am* disappointed."

Darya's anger returned, hotter than ever. "*You're* disappointed? *I'm* disappointed! You *left* us, Mama! And for the longest time, I thought it was my fault, because of that stupid riddle. 'If I ask you a riddle and you don't get it, then will you stay?'" Her voice hitched. "Do you remember that?"

Mama looked startled, and then guilty. Her eyes darted from side to side.

324

"You do!" Darya cried. "And you said, 'Sure, honey, give it your best shot.' I was five years old!"

"I'm fairly certain I didn't say, 'Sure, honey, give it your best shot,'" Mama said.

Darya shook her head. "You left, and I thought it was my fault. Then you came back, and . . . you made me buy cigarettes! So guess what? I don't have to listen to you!" She scrambled off her bed and ran for the door.

"Darya, wait!" Mama wailed. She followed Darya out of the room. "I know I messed up. I came back *because* I messed up. Darya!"

Darya's bare feet drummed the stairs. She heard Mama behind her, but she was younger and faster and more agile. She swung herself around the round wooden knob on the corner of the stair railing and dashed down the hall, through the mudroom, and out the back door, which banged shut behind her.

Was Mama still chasing after her? Darya's blood was pounding so loudly in her head that she didn't know. There could have been a wolf on her heels and she might not have known, or the flapping wings of a giant owl, or a lion or tiger or bear.

In front of her was Papa's workshop, but even in her panic, she was smart enough to veer to the left. No way was she leading Mama straight to Papa's door. She ran half a mile before slowing to a jog, then a walk, and then dropping down and collapsing against the trunk of an oak tree. Her breaths were ragged. Her feet felt tender, and when she examined them, the welling of small cuts and gashes made her wince.

Someone cleared her throat.

"Who's there?" Darya said. She peered around the tree trunk.

"Such a drama queen," the Bird Lady scolded.

"No," Darya moaned. "No, no, no, no, no."

She blinked hard, but when she checked again, the Bird Lady was still there. She sported a sombrero with small felt balls dangling from the rim. Also, a pantsuit made of stretchy yarn pot holders stitched together. Also, white go-go boots.

Darya rather liked the go-go boots, actually. Then she remembered how much everything sucked and returned to scorning them.

"What do you want?" she said.

"To help you," the Bird Lady said.

"Oh? By whipping up some chips and guac?"

The Bird Lady gave her a look, and Darya huffed. The sweat she'd worked up was cooling. She shivered in her tank top.

"Would you rather mope and stew for a week—or a month or a year—before figuring out how to move forward?" the Bird Lady said. "If so, that's your choice. But what if the world moves on without you?"

"Then the world moves on without me." Darya scowled. "What say do I have over anything, anyway?"

"Perhaps not much, perhaps enough," the Bird Lady acknowledged.

Darya rolled her eyes.

"Listen, pet. The world doesn't always make sense, but you can still love it."

"Oh, wow. You should write bumper stickers. Have you ever thought of that?"

The Bird Lady waited.

Darya groaned and pulled her feet toward her so that she was sitting crisscross applesauce. She tucked her toes into the warm folds of her knees. "Fine. How can I love the world even when it doesn't make sense?"

"By loving one of its beings," answered the Bird Lady.

"Oh, well, sure. *That*. What happens when one of those 'beings' doesn't love you back? What if there used to be love, but . . . it left?"

She heard the Bird Lady sigh. Then she heard scooching noises, fabric on soil. The Bird Lady settled in beside her, the warmth of her body not unwelcome. She said, "Stitch it back up."

"Huh?"

"The broken thread. Stitch it back up."

"I don't understand."

"We humans are part of the universe," the Bird Lady said. "Don't you see that? We might sometimes *feel* separated, but that's an illusion. A broken thread. So, stitch it back up."

Darya closed her eyes and leaned the back of her head against the oak tree.

"There is a poet," the Bird Lady said. "His name is Rumi. Would you like to know what he said?"

*Not if it's in the form of a poem*, Darya thought.

The Bird Lady waited.

"Sure," Darya said. "Whatever."

"'Out beyond ideas of wrongdoing and rightdoing, there is a field. I'll meet you there.'" The Bird Lady patted Darya's knee.

"Terrific," Darya said. "What does it mean?"

"Oh, dear one," the Bird Lady said. Her head touched Darya's, and Darya wondered if she would wake up tomorrow and find a sparrow in her hair.

"Transformation is a wondrous thing, but it's not always pleasant for the person who's transforming."

"You make it sound like I'm a butterfly trying to burst out of my cocoon," Darya said.

"Who said you're the butterfly?"

"I'm not? Then who is?"

The Bird Lady squeezed Darya's knee, then patted it and struggled to her feet. Her voice seemed to come from far away, and her words were like mushy fruit. "Just remember one thing."

"What's that?"

"Just because you don't have wings, that doesn't mean you can't fly."

# CHAPTER THIRTY-THREE

With December came the first snowfall, and Darya wondered if it could be a new beginning.

"It snowed, it snowed!" Ava caroled, barreling into Darya's room and launching herself onto Darya's bed.

"Too early," Darya groaned. She tried to burrow back into her dream—something about a field of poppies and dozens of fluttering butterflies—but Ava pulled Darya's forearm from her eyes.

"Get up! Come see! It's beautiful!" She scrambled behind Darya and pushed her, leaning back on her palms and driving her heels into Darya's bottom.

Darya slid off her bed and landed hard on the

floor. "Ow," she complained.

But she let Ava help her to her feet and drag her across the room. At the window, Ava stopped babbling. She stood by Darya, their shoulders touching. Everything was hushed. Everything was pure. The world was cloaked in dazzling promise.

Something swelled in Darya's chest. Something big. She shooed Ava out, saying, "It *is* beautiful. Thanks for showing me. Now go away, please—and maybe ask Aunt Vera to make waffles?"

The moment Ava was gone, Darya got to work. She'd been thinking about this for almost two weeks now. What to do about Mama, and possibly Emily and Tally, too. She dragged her box of puzzles from her closet. She carefully removed Tally's taped-together drawing. Then she spilled the scraps of paper with riddles and picture puzzles on them onto the carpet.

She once knew how to make origami birds. She suspected she still could.

She gathered other supplies as well. A story had sprung to her mind, and she wanted to capture it somehow. Not as a drawing, but something like a drawing.

She worked all morning, cutting and pasting and gluing. She arranged objects only to frown and rearrange them. At some point Ava must have brought her a waffle, and at some point Darya must have wolfed it down, because later she pushed her hair off her face and ended up with a smear of syrup across her cheek.

*Huh*, she thought, taking in the sticky plate a few feet away from her. Never in her life had she gotten so absorbed in something that she failed to notice a waffle making its way into her room, not to mention her stomach. Was this what it was like for Tally, when she got lost in her art?

Darya hoped she'd told Ava thank you, and that she'd asked Ava to tell Aunt Vera thanks as well.

Around noon, she scrapped everything she'd done and started over, and to her surprise, she didn't beat herself up over it. Instead of getting frustrated, or giving up, she simply began again.

After she secured the last origami bird, she put the lid on the shoebox. She covered the edge of the lid with a ribbon and glued the ribbon in place. She covered the rest of the shoebox with pale green tissue paper, hiding the Adidas slogan. She leaned back on her heels and nodded.

From the outside, it looked like a pretty box and nothing more.

But on the inside . . .

She wiggled onto her tummy and pressed her eye

to the hole she'd cut into the side of the box. Paper birds swayed from a foil-lined sky, held in place with snippets of thread that were nearly invisible. A spray of tissue paper poppies stretched across a bed of Easter basket grass, each flower stained the color of berries from being held, one by one, to Darya's berry red lips.

She'd fashioned a tree out of a wire hanger, which she'd covered in fake fur clipped from the hood and cuffs of an old jacket. Wedged within its branches was a cutout figure of a girl, safe from the blowing wind because there was no wind. Not inside the box.

Behind the tree stood two other paper doll girls, positioned to show that they were holding hands.

At the very back of the box, pressed into the corner, was a larger cutout. A Mama paper doll. Darya had considered leaving her face a blank slate. She almost did. Then she thought of Emily, and Tally, and— strangely—Papa.

Carefully, she'd folded Tally's picture of her mother to show only Tally's mother's face, and this she secured into place above the other mother's body.

Darya gazed into the box for several minutes. It wasn't perfect, but it would do.

She told Aunt Vera that the box was a school project and that she had to take it to Tally's house, because it was Tally's job to do the finishing touches.

"What kind of project?" Aunt Vera asked. "It looks like a box to me."

"Yeah, that's why I'm taking it to Tally," Darya fibbed. "She'll make it better. Tally's a really good artist."

Aunt Vera sniffed. "Not as good as you, I'm sure."

"No, she's way better. Her art . . . it's like her way of seeing the world, and then I see things in new ways, too. Like what the truth might be, you know?"

"I don't, to be honest. But if you say so."

"I do," Darya said.

Soon, depending on what she found out from Mama, Darya would have a truth to give to Tally. It would most likely be a very small truth, a sliver that reinforced the not-knowing-ness that already existed.

But . . . maybe not.

She pieced together what she knew about Tally's mom: She'd been a lonely teenager, no family to speak of, obsessed with orphans and children thrown out on their own. She'd grown into a young woman, and then a young woman with a child.

In the photograph Tally had redrawn, the little

girl—Tally—had looked to be four or five, the same age Darya had been when Mama left. Tally's mother, in the picture, had looked to be in her late twenties, the same age as Mama when Mama left.

And, Mama's Emily had been an artist, just like Tally was an artist.

The pieces *could* fit. They didn't *not* fit.

If it was the *right* fit—unlikely, but if—then the information Darya gave Tally would be a very large truth. It would change Tally's world, and Darya's too. Emily would have her family back. Tally would have three cousins.

The Tally piece of all this would come later, however. Today was about Mama. She'd looked up the address of Aunt Elena's charming garage apartment, and as she walked there through the snow, she held her dreamscape carefully in front of her. Every so often, she paused and peeked through the eyehole for courage.

When she passed the tree where she'd last seen the Bird Lady, she stopped and called out, "Hey! Are you here?"

She sensed movement from within the woods, several yards from the trail. The Bird Lady emerged, swaddled in a puffy yellow coat that made her look like a dandelion. Her hat was white and fluffy, with a pom-pom on top. Her eyes were merry.

"I need to ask you something, and I really hope you'll give me a straight answer," Darya said. "It has to do with the Forgetting Spell."

"Ah yes, I remember."

"Ha ha, very clever," Darya said. She swallowed. "I wanted to forget about letting Mama get away. Right?"

The Bird Lady stepped closer. "You wanted to forget who you were. You almost succeeded."

Darya shuddered. "Well . . . that's creepy. But the spell—has it been lifted?"

The Bird Lady didn't answer. She'd slipped back into the woods, moving so fluidly that all Darya saw was a golden blur.

"Hey! When will I see you again?"

No answer.

"Where do you sleep when it's cold like this? Will you be warm enough?"

No answer.

"Fine, but listen. If you need anything, will you tell me? Please? Because . . . I can help!"

Darya heard the words come out of her mouth, and she knew them to be genuine. She marveled at the strangeness of it. The Darya from before her birthday was different from the Darya of last week, and Darya from last week was different from Darya today.

She wanted to remember them all. She also wanted to keep changing—and growing—until the end of her days.

When she rang the doorbell to her aunt's apartment, it was Ava who let her in.

"Darya!" she exclaimed. "How did you know we'd be here?"

"I didn't, but I thought you might."

Ava's face lit up, and she turned to the others, who were sitting around the table in a small, cozy kitchen. "Natasha, it's Darya! Mama! It's *Darya*!"

Mama pushed back her chair and stood up.

Tears sprang to Darya's eyes, totally without her permission. She blinked them away and thrust out the box. "Here," she said. "This is for you."

Mama stepped forward and took it. Her lower lip trembled, until she pressed both lips together to control it. "Thank you."

"You're welcome, but you might not like it," Darya said. "It's not all sunshine and sparkles."

"I wouldn't expect it to be," Mama said, and something loosened in Darya's chest.

"Come sit down," Aunt Elena said. Her cheeks were pink and her hair tumbled around her face. "Would you like some hot chocolate?"

"Yes . . . I think . . . but I have to say something first."

Then Mama nodded. She still hadn't peered into the box. She might not have spotted the eyehole, even.

Darya lifted her chin. "I wished to have nothing to do with you. That was the wish I could make come true myself, and I did."

Mama didn't interrupt.

"But it's up to me whether I let it keep being true," Darya went on, "and I don't want to anymore."

"What are you saying?" Ava said. "Are you saying what I think you're saying?"

Darya locked her gaze on Mama. "I'm saying . . . yes. I want you back in my life. On one condition."

"What's that, sweetie?"

"Don't call me sweetie," Darya said. "Wait—that's not the condition. That's just . . . don't, please. I don't even know you."

"Darya," Aunt Elena said.

"No, Elena, it's fine," Mama said. "What's the condition?"

"That you tell Papa."

The color drained from Mama's face.

"That you tell *everybody*," Darya said. Her heart hammered. "That you let *us* tell everybody. That you stop being a secret. That's the condition."

Mama's eyes grew round and scared. She glanced at the door, and Darya thought, *What have I done? She's going to run.*

Natasha stood up.

Aunt Elena stood up.

Ava, who was already standing, stepped closer. She said, "She's right, Mama. We all want that."

Mama's chest rose and fell.

"So will you?" Darya said, and her voice did that quivery thing she hated.

Several long seconds passed.

"I'll try," Mama said.

She put the dreamscape box on the counter, but she didn't take Darya's hands or hug her or force some grand moment. She simply held Darya's gaze, nothing between them but possibility.

*Tally.*
*Tally.*
*Tally.*
—Emily Striker, age thirty-five

# ACKNOWLEDGMENTS

SO many hugs and thank-yous to my editor, Claudia Gabel, and to her editor-buddy, Alex Arnold, who by the lucky winds of fate served as Claudia's coconspirator. You ladies have taught me so much—and always with grace, kindness, and the clear shining generosity of brilliance. I am one lucky author. Thanks to Anica Rissi for having such fab ideas, and thanks as well to Katherine Tegen and all the players on her all-star team. Thanks for inviting me to play. It is a privilege.

Thanks to Bob, always, and special thanks to Emily Lockhart and Sarah Mlynowski for relentlessly cheering me on, whether on the topic of writing, beauty products, or overall life philosophies. Thanks, too, to Pamela Bantham, Jenny McLean, and Melyssa Mead for the laughs, the tears, the cocktails.

Thanks to Ruth and Tim White, Don and Sarah Lee Myracle, and my many sisters and brothers for being awesome.

Same for my kiddos. I love you!

And a bottomless well of gratitude, appreciation, and mushy love for my husband, Randy Bartels, who brings joy to my life every second of every day. You, Randy, are my magic.